Dead Territory

A Tale of Gangs, Police, and Betrayal

By

D. C. Tucker

Disclaimer

This novel is a work of fiction inspired in part by the author's background in policing. The characters, incidents and organisations portrayed are wholly products of the author's imagination. Any resemblance to real persons, living or deceased, or to actual events, is unintended and coincidental.

Dedication

To Nic, Louis and Jacey.

Acknowledgments

In memory of Jim Tucker, also known as Bill James, author of the Harpur and Iles series of novels, and of my mother, Marian.

About the Author

D. C. Tucker served as a police officer for over thirty years. During his time on the force he served on the Metropolitan Police's firearms unit and worked in counter terrorism.

This novel draws on firsthand experience of crime and policing in the early 1980s, exploring the moral grey areas faced by officers on both sides of the law.

Dead Territory —the first of his novels set in the world of Bill James's acclaimed Harpur & Iles series—is a taut, uncompromising study of power, loyalty, and corruption.

D. C. Tucker is the youngest son of Bill James.

Contents

Chapter 1

Copsey felt safe here. It was a derelict house. The windows had been broken years ago and the frames taken for firewood. The doors had suffered a similar fate, dark doorways left, threateningly inviting. Many of the stairs and floorboards had also burned in a harsh winter, but enough remained for an agile drug addict to find his way to his safe place. He could shoot up safe from detection by the cops: going into this house would breach their health and safety assessment. The only visitors would be other addicts looking for their safe place and to share needles and syringes. Brotherhood and sisterhood in hopelessness.

It was cold and the sky was heavy with suffocating cloud. The late afternoon light was seeping away. It was trying to rain but didn't seem to have enough energy to manage it. Copsey had spent most of his adult life coping with changes in weather, so he was used to being cold. The house still had most of its roof and, in any event, rain was no concern to a hardened street dweller like him.

He had gone up to the first floor, where the large rooms would once have housed well-off shipowners and their families. Copsey gazed out of the window at the front garden and street. He absorbed the calm given off by the chaos: discarded rubbish, black refuse sacks, piles of broken bricks and concrete, abandoned skips, a burnt-out Ford Anglia, the proceeds of a joyride. Anything that might have contained food had been ripped open and scavenged by hungry wildlife. It was all derelictly still. He could hold on a bit longer, anticipating the warmth of the high, the detachment from reality, the moments of serenity.

Copsey had just managed to sell some LPs he'd stolen and had immediately spent the money on a small wrap of heroin, purchased from his usual dealer, Justin Paynter. He'd keep a bit back to sell on to a lightweight user; someone looking for a high but without the experience of a hardcore addict, someone young and middle class. He'd cut it with something to make it look like a full deal. Then he'd buy another wrap. No thought of food; there were more important things.

The stillness was disturbed by two men walking up the street. They looked straight at him, seeing him framed in the window. They hurried towards the door, stepping around the various obstructions. Copsey didn't recognise these two but they didn't look like the normal Esplanade clientele; they looked too healthy to be dealers or addicts, and they weren't with a woman, so not pimps or clients. Their clothing was too clean and unholed. He felt uneasy; his safe place was no longer safe.

He left the front room and went to hide in a room towards the back of the house. He found a room with some geriatric mattresses and a collapsing sofa. He lay on the floor behind the sofa and pulled the mattress over him. He lay still and listened, hoping they would go somewhere else. He knew his hiding place was hopeless.

He could hear the heavy steps of the two as they navigated the stairs.

'Jesus, Copsey… this place is a death trap. Come out and say hello.'

Copsey decided against waiting for them to find him. One of the other rooms had a window that looked out over the remains of a porch roof that had protected the rear door. Most of the tiles had gone, but some of the supporting woodwork remained and might hold his weight if he jumped out. He wasn't inclined to find out whether the two men were planning a social visit.

He shuffled out from under the mattress and tiptoed onto the landing. As he reached the door to the other room, the two men reached the top of the stairs and saw him. He ran into the room and looked down through the missing window. The porch looked considerably less robust than he remembered, and it was a bigger drop. Time to decide—jump and hope, or try to dodge them? He jumped.

The porch roof collapsed as if it weren't there. He landed heavily on abandoned rubble. The porch had thrown him off and he landed on his side. He had a few cuts and scrapes, but nothing he hadn't dealt with before. His knee took most of his weight when he landed. He hobbled off as quickly as he could, somewhere between walking, running and stumbling, stepping carefully between the piles of rubble. The abandoned masonry tripped him as he struggled to lift his injured leg. He looked back and saw the men at the window. They weren't going to jump.

They looked out of the window and then disappeared back inside. They picked their way carefully over the missing and rotting boards, emerging from the house but not seeing Copsey anywhere.

One said to the other, 'He's gone to ground in one of these houses. You stay here, make sure he doesn't get back out here without us knowing. I'll look through the houses. I like hide and seek. This will be fun.'

As Copsey tried to move silently around the deserted house, the years of decay conspired to reveal his every move: the crack of a rotten floorboard here, the squelch of a sodden mattress there. The bare walls and floors acted like amplifiers, echoing every sound to every corner.

'Alfred,' called one, 'I've got Copsey over here. Come and join the party.'

Copsey ran towards the back of the house as best he could on his crocked knee. The pain didn't penetrate the panic in his mind, but his knee wouldn't support a speedy ascent. As he reached the stairs, he felt a strong grip take hold of his arm and he was yanked backwards down the stairs.

Copsey wriggled and writhed, hoping to get free. Even if he could, he wasn't sure what he would do. Running was futile; he was too addled and injured to stay upright unaided. As he was pushed along, he tripped and tumbled over the accumulated filth of years but was supported by a strong arm. He felt that he ought to show some resistance, but the man had a good grip on his arm and then pushed him forcefully against a wall. Copsey's head snapped back and hit the wall, releasing a cascade of dust.

'I'm on my way to you now, Robin.'

Copsey thought they didn't look like an Alfred and a Robin. They looked far too much like people who'd had difficult upbringings, and people like that weren't called Alfred or Robin. He also thought the names might be a joke—Batman-related names. Robin certainly didn't act like a caped crusader. Alfred did have a big fleshy face, like a cartoon character: oversized lips beneath a bulbous nose and a heavy brow.

Copsey had once been a healthy six-footer but was now thin, an almost translucent tracing of his former self. His movements were inhibited by tremors. He was dressed in jeans that clung grimly to the remains of his buttocks, the seat material hanging behind his thighs. The filthy padded anorak was saved from showing the dirt by being black. His dreadlocks retained pieces of fluff and straw, some embedded fairly recently.

'Jesus, when did you last have a shower?' asked Alfred, but he wasn't interested in the response.

'What's happening?' asked Copsey.

Alfred, who seemed to be the chatty one, said, 'Our employer wants us to send a message to your employer.' He drew out a gold packet of Benson & Hedges, put a cigarette between his lips and struck a match. He cupped the flame between his hands, protecting it from the wind. He took a deep draw and exhaled forcefully. The smoke formed a momentary cloud before being whisked away on the stiff breeze.

Copsey was confused for a moment; he wasn't employed and hadn't been for years. Who'd employ him?

'Guys, there's no need for nastiness. I can carry a message for you to whoever you like. I'm well known around here, sort of respected. I speak to lots of people. I'll speak to anyone you like and can definitely get over the seriousness you'd want, yes definitely.'

'Unfortunately, that's not how this particular message is to be given, although you will be the messenger. It's just business,' Alfred replied.

With that, they put the hapless Copsey on the floor. Robin held one arm still while Alfred took a needle and syringe from his pocket and injected the contents into Copsey's pockmarked arm.

Copsey felt the familiar warmth of his skin as the heroin hit, but that was all he felt.

They loaded Copsey into the boot of their car and drove around aimlessly, waiting for time to pass, to let the evening punters get off home so they wouldn't be disturbed.

All natural light had gone and the wet roads were just about illuminated by the orange streetlights. They parked at the end of an alleyway. It looked very similar to where they had found Copsey, strewn with the evidence of decay and neglect.

Alfred and Robin picked up Copsey and picked their way down the alleyway, away from the streetlights. They placed him in a disused garage. The once robust wooden doors were now sagging on their hinges, jammed on the ground. Inside were the essentials of the visitors—discarded drugs kit and used condoms. They put Copsey on his back, arranged the drug paraphernalia and left.

Alfred said, 'Message ends.'

***

Benny Loxton sat in the front room of his two-up two-down terraced house on the Floss Estate. He had purchased some upmarket, leather-bound furniture that was too large for the room. The space between each luxurious piece was a little small, making the already small room even smaller.

He had recently redecorated using wallpaper that had a mixture of brightly coloured squares and rectangles; he had been told that they were 'geometric shapes.' He liked the sound of the words. They were intelligent-sounding.

Benny was in his early thirties and his hair was beginning to show signs of thinning and receding. Long slivers of skin crept up the sides of his forehead. For the moment there was no need for a comb-over, but the time for it was rushing on.

He was wearing a silk shirt and expensive-looking trousers. The clothing was at odds with the face that wore the signs of many battles, not all won. He was drawing on a Rothmans.

'So this is a message to me?'

Sid Lycette and Phil Macey sat opposite Benny in one of the large leather armchairs. Lycette was younger than Benny and clearly not aspiring to the same class of living. He wore old jeans, a nearly white T-shirt and a well-worn pair of white Adidas Samba trainers. They'd have looked great when new.

'That's what I were told. I were checking on trade around the Esplanade. A few of our traders were a bit cut up about Copsey. They'd heard that someone was upset about him trading out of the Esplanade and that there had to be a clear message. They was worried that they could be next. I told them they'd be fine on the Esplanade, that you'd look after them and that you've got lots of people to keep an eye out and make sure there's no disruption.'

Macey was wearing wide-flared jeans and a long-sleeved shirt with a bright floral pattern. He had a mop of fair hair; he looked like he hadn't quite made the transition from the 1970s into the 1980s.

'We can't let this go unanswered. We got to do something.'

'Do we know who is sending the message? Do we know what the message is?' Benny asked.

Lycette replied, 'Well, I think the message is clear: don't trade on someone else's ground. Trouble is, we don't know who and we don't know where.'

Loxton added, 'Phil, I love your willingness to take action, but it can be a problem, as we all know. Do what? Who against?'

Loxton threw his head back on the chair and looked at the ceiling, seeking inspiration.

'This is fucking stupid. It feels like someone has decided that there should be areas set aside for the different teams. No one has ever suggested that before. How are we supposed to play by the rules if we don't know what the rules are? And we don't know who is making the fucking rules! This isn't fucking Monopoly. Nobody writes the rules.' He stubbed his cigarette out vigorously.

Lycette spoke softly, 'Well, we've always operated in and around the Esplanade. Maybe someone has assumed, wrongly, that this was our turf and that everywhere else is someone else's?'

Macey, speaking less softly, added, 'Let's get after Tacette. It's probably him.'

Loxton nodded. 'It's got to be Tacette, hasn't it? Who else? Phil's right; we can't let this go. We need to think of a suitable reply to his message.'

***

In her south London flat, Elspeth Marie Philipson was talking to Alfred and Robin. Copsey had been right; they weren't called Alfred and Robin. Jason Jenner Meredith, the chatty one, wore jeans and a T-shirt, showing off his well-developed biceps and the overly colourful tattoo of a tiger on his right arm. Robin, now reverting to his given name of Leonard Barry Calvin, was also dressed casually in jeans and a T-shirt, but his less developed arms didn't fill the short sleeves as well as his colleague's. Calvin's nose followed a serpentine route down his face and there were off-white lines of scar tissue above his eyes and across his cheeks, a face that had lived some sort of life.

Meredith was describing events. 'Else, it went like a dream. Exactly what we expected and planned. We found him easily enough in the usual rundown place he was squatting in. He tried to run but we caught him easy. We didn't have to wait no time because he was on his lonesome.'

Calvin, feeling the need to impress, added, 'I found him, and he tried to run up some stairs. Once I'd got hold of him, he wasn't going nowhere.'

'Then we just drove around with him in the boot. He was the quietest backseat driver I've ever had.' Meredith laughed at his own joke.

He continued, 'When it was quiet, we put him in a disused garage and then phoned the Old Bill from a phone box. We left him face up, eyes open, with the drug paraphernalia next to him.'

Else was in her mid-thirties and had retained the figure of her youth. She was around average height, with a pretty but hard face: narrow eyes and well-defined cheekbones and nose. She had good taste in make-up and used enough to bring out her best points without making it overdone. She was dressed in a smart trouser suit with a white blouse.

'So, it's all gone well. The cops will think it's an overdose, and even if they don't, they're not going to be bothered by the death of a black, drug-addicted nobody. And no family connected enough to make a big noise about it. It would be a fucking cheek if they did, eh? They've practically abandoned him for years. If they want to kick up a fuss, the first question everyone will ask is, "Where were you when he needed help?" It's practically a victimless crime.'

'Apart from the victim.' Calvin observed.

Meredith said, 'Else, that was a good choice of yours and a brilliant and clear way to send a message to Loxton. He's got to wind his neck in and keep his dealing to his side of the street.'

Else said, 'Daryl is very keen to expand into new areas outside London. Our job is to carve out our new area and make sure the locals know that there's a new, big player in town. I'm not sure that we have been clear enough yet and we may need to do a bit more message sending soon.'

Calvin shifted in his seat. 'Else, that's all well and good. But they're not going to just sit there and let us move in. We'll need to be ready for a bit of a battle.'

Else replied, 'Leave the thinking to me and Daryl; we've gone through all the scenarios. We've got all the people and equipment we need. This lot are countryside nobodies. They don't know what it's like to have some real big-city operators next to them. We'll be very reasonable. Let them keep some of their existing territory.

When we're settled there, we can expand and push them right out.
Should be lots of money to be made.'

Meredith and Calvin laughed out loud. Meredith began singing 'My
Way' and Calvin joined in.

Chapter 2

Iles looked around his new office, a symphony of dull corporate blue, with the title 'Supt – Corporate Affairs' on the door. He wondered how public bodies were so adept at sucking the life out of colour.

He was wearing one of his best bespoke suits. The material complemented his tall, lean figure and angular face. The suit was a luxurious wool of deep, deep blue. His silk red tie was bright enough to fight its corner with the magnificent suit. His Italian shoes were highly polished. His black, tightly curled hair was well cut and showing the first signs of grey around his ears. He exuded relaxed intensity.

Chief Constable Barton walked in, dressed in uniform. He was short for a cop, around five foot eight, and had the figure of a man who had spent too much time at a desk. He looked a little unkempt as his shirt navigated his girth and overhung his trousers, which seemed to be pulled too tight—an effort, perhaps, to convince himself that he was a size smaller than he actually was.

He sat, uninvited, on the one fairly comfortable chair.

'It's great to see you again, Des. Reminds me of those days getting after that gang. We've both come some distance since then.'

'Yes, I look back on those days with fondness. The ability to operate effectively against criminals with the public supportive and political oversight non-existent. Some of the things we did then we can no longer do. I remember the time when we—'

The chief wriggled in his chair and cut in. 'Yes, best to leave those things in the past, gathering some dust. We've moved on and face a different challenge now. I've asked the ACC to brief you on your task here because I've got to go to a meeting with the local authority; they like me to be in uniform.'

Iles replied, 'We'll leave the murky past in the murky past, but I always think it useful to remember how effective we can be in policing when we focus ruthlessly on combating crime and criminals.'

***

ACC Davies-Hywel walked in. He was a small man with wispy, disappearing hair. What remained was carefully placed to cover as much of the pate as possible. He had a pinched, angular face, as if permanently sucking on a lime. He was in uniform, white shirt with his crossed tipstaves badges of rank on the black epaulettes. His skinny, pale arms hung out of his short-sleeved shirt. He was wearing the extra braids of his rank on his collar.

'Welcome to the force, Superintendent,' Davies-Hywel said with barely disguised insincerity. He held onto the 's' of superintendent, sounding like a pantomime snake. He smiled with his mouth.

'I understand that you know the chief of old. He sees in you the particular skills and attributes needed to drive through a customer-focused approach to policing in this force.' With each sibilant sound, the elongated 's.'

Iles leant back in his chair, allowing his trouser leg to rise and reveal a bright yellow sock. Davies-Hywel glanced and recoiled as if he had seen an affront to his most fundamental values.

'I expect you'll want to wear your uniform as and when you've been kitted out. I'm very keen on our senior officers being visible—in uniform.'

'You can be sure I'll be visible in uniform,' Iles replied.

Davies-Hywel continued, 'And I put great store in the traditional values of audit and compliance, Superintendent. As the lead for corporate affairs, you will no doubt share my zeal for making sure we do the basics right in this force. Yes, audit and compliance are the building blocks of excellent policing; I'm sure you'll agree.'

'It's certainly possible,' Iles replied.

'What is?'

'That I'll agree.'

'My sources tell me of some serious allegations concerning you in your old force, and I'd certainly not wish to see any of that controversy here.' All the sibilant sounds seemed to join like air leaking from a tyre.

'Yes, I think I can claim some modest successes in dealing with a few bottom feeders. The trouble with some in policing today is that they've forgotten their powers to intervene to stop criminals from operating. I'm sure you'll want to tell me of some of your conspicuous victories against the foul-smelling detritus you've encountered here. I'd love to hear of your last arrest, so I can fully understand the value that compliance and audit added. I think that's the new lingua franca, "value added." I'm struggling to understand how looking at bureaucracy helps in the fight against the tide of fucking filth that blights our society. I, for one, see it as my mission to make the place better. It's almost a divine calling for me. I find that a robust, unflinching approach to those who would disturb peace and tranquillity often delivers results, even if that approach can sometimes tread close to the limits of traditional policing. I think it's somewhere in the Bible: "When justice is done, it is a joy to the righteous but terror to evildoers." I'm particularly keen on the terror to evildoers bit.'

'Yes, that's what I'd heard.' Davies-Hywel walked out, back to the safety of his own office.

***

Iles went for a stroll around HQ. The lank blueness pervaded everywhere and there was a smell of paint—new chief, new paint job. He came to a door marked 'DI – Care.' He knocked and went in.

'Jesus, that's a job you've got there… or is that your name?'

DI Colin Harpur peered around a tower of papers. Some were in thick files with flat, neutral covers containing years of accumulated information that some poor sod would have to review—in this case, Harpur.

'Not exactly the job I'd hoped for, but someone's got to do it. Anything that isn't viewed as real policing but has the potential to drop someone in deep, deep shit is my job. Or am I sounding a bit cynical?'

Harpur was an imposing physical specimen, his body fighting to break free from the confines of his ill-fitting suit. A mop of unruly fair hair jostled on his head above a big face that was handsome in its own, unique way, reminiscent of over-promoted British heavyweight boxers.

Iles introduced himself.

Harpur said, 'Yes, I'd heard you were joining us.'

'I'd have thought you might try to dress up a bit for a new senior officer. I can see that M&S are doing quite well from you. Trouble is, they weren't thinking of someone of your shape when they were cutting the material. Looks like you've got plenty on your desk.'

Harpur replied, 'Yes, a gift from my predecessor. I'm going through them all, and this one's a report about the death of a drug addict.'

'Is that "caring"?'

'Not really, but anything involving stuff no one else wants to deal with is my responsibility, it would seem. I'm just lucky like that. Black kid died of a drugs overdose. Lots of injuries on the body, but put down to a chaotic lifestyle—good police jargon to cover a load of unexplained messiness. If no one cares, no one is going to ask the questions.'

Iles asked, 'What's your hypothesis; that's the teaching these days: form a number of hypotheses and see how the evidence stacks up.'

'That's the problem—the initial report is poor. There's no photography and no decent scene description. And it's a couple of weeks old, so the scene won't hold much for us now.'

'Family?'

Harpur replied, 'He was disconnected from them for several years. The local force informed his parents. They haven't called us for details, so I think we're unlikely to get any inconvenient harassment from them. Death is so final. Families can be very difficult; they want meaning from the death of a loved one, the feeble cry that this must never happen to anyone else. We know, of course, that it will happen to someone else. It might be classified in a different way to make it seem as if it hasn't happened again, but we know it has, and it will again.'

Iles said, 'You've got quite a dose of cynicism there. But, then again, nobody's going to give a flying fuck about a dead druggy, so no hurry.'

Harpur nodded, closed the file, and moved to the next one in the pile.

Chapter 3

Chief Constable Barton walked into Iles' office.

'Des, it's great to see you again. Your reputation has followed you here. I'm hoping that you're going to bring your unorthodox approach to crime fighting and use it to improve the force. I see this as my challenge here, moving to a more customer-focused approach, where policing adds value to every interaction. I think Locard's principle has greater application than just at crime scenes. Every time the police interact with someone, there should be a positive impact—maybe Newton's third law is more apposite than Locard; every action should create a better and more positive reaction. Do you see how these ideas of physics can be applied to policing?'

Iles exclaimed, 'Your reputation precedes you too and, as always, you bring unrivalled insight. I can't wait to get started. I've already spoken to the ACC, who was ever so supportive. He spoke of the value of audit and compliance, things that have always been close to my heart.'

The chief held his gaze on Iles, looking for signs of sarcasm, but none were detected.

Iles spotted Harpur in the corridor.

'Sorry to leave you, but I'm keen to be seen out and about, and DI Harpur is just leaving the station. I would welcome the opportunity to see some operational work—you know, to get a sense of how things are done here.'

'Excellent, excellent. Just what I want to hear. You're looking to turn over a few stones and see what's hidden. I'm relying on you to be the cleanser, the person who drives and enables a new approach. "Wash and make yourselves clean. Take your evil deeds out of my sight; stop doing wrong." I'll supply the vision; you supply the implementation—one of my favourite words.'

Iles broke into a fast walk and caught up with Harpur at the top of the stairs.

'Mind if I join you?'

'Not at all, but it may not be very interesting. You remember the druggie death I was looking at? Has all the potential to drop us in it should anyone decide to care. Have you yet caught up with the policing lead from the council? A guy called Jeavons? Very big on the unfortunates in society—beaten-up wives, neglected children, gays, lesbians, blacks, browns—you name it, he's concerned. This is the type of case that could ring his bell, so I thought it a good idea to appear interested. I'm popping down to look at the scene. There'll be nothing there now, two weeks after he was found, but I like to get a feel for where things have happened.'

'How very noble of Jeavons. I expect that he and I might have some interesting conversations about policing priorities.'

They passed the door to the canteen. A gale of fag smoke flowed out as an officer went in. They went down the concrete steps into the station yard.

Harpur took a shabby off-white Vauxhall Viva from the pool. The cops seemed to have a particular skill in obtaining cars in colours that no one in their right mind would buy. Iles looked somewhat out of place in his shining suit. Harpur looked somewhat out of place as his large form filled the car and made it look like he was wearing it.

Harpur asked, without looking away from the road, 'Corporate affairs—doesn't sound like a job you'd welcome.'

Iles said, 'Why do you say that?'

Harpur responded, 'If the rumours from your previous force are true, I'd have thought that you'd prefer something more hands-on.'

'Are you taking the piss? The only people who want corporate affairs jobs are office dwellers, people with shiny arses, polished from sitting down all day. If your sources are any good, you'll know I'm here on loan because it suits everyone. I took an uncompromising approach to the villains of my previous patch and, to quote Corporal Jones, they didn't like it up 'em.'

Harpur laughed. 'I've found they don't want to play by the rules but get upset when others don't play by the rules. I suppose it's one of the reasons we never win the war; we do tend to follow the rules, mainly, whilst our enemies don't, and then have lawyers to pick their way through all the information we've given them to find the holes. We'll win some battles, but the war? It can never be won.'

'But that's what we love, the hopeless pursuit of glory. There's an endless stream of the lawless, often from the same families, evolving in an uncontrolled way. It's like trying to fight a particularly virulent form of cancer. We might be able to cut some bits off, but it will keep growing back in new forms and in different places. Christ, it sounds bloody hopeless, but we love it.'

Harpur parked on the high street and hoped his inconspicuous car would not draw attention and he could visit the scene of the death unnoticed. The Superintendent, resplendent in his peacock clothing, wasn't helping with the inconspicuousness he craved. The

Esplanade had once been an upmarket area where wealthy shipowners had their properties, to be close to the docks so that they could oversee the loading and unloading of valuable cargoes. These days, the docks had become redundant, like so many of the people who had worked there. The houses of the Esplanade had been divided and sub-divided and sometimes abandoned so that increasingly impoverished people could live there.

'Gold' by Spandau Ballet was on the car radio. The new romantic image and song were somewhat at odds with the Esplanade, but maybe hinted towards better days ahead.

The quality of the upkeep reflected the changes in clientele: no one with the money to paint doors and window frames, pay for the window cleaners or replace the threadbare curtains. No sign of the gold that was once there and was remembered by Spandau Ballet. It had all moved into the pockets of the bankers.

Some of the shops were unoccupied—the creeping ghost town. The shops that remained had brightly lit frontages of primary colours, projecting glamour and hope whilst purveying cheap fast food and booze for the unglamorous and hopeless. Above the shops were flats, some occupied, others long, long abandoned. The dreary, overcast sky filled everywhere, leaching heat and light.

They walked down a poorly maintained alley behind a row of shops. The rubbish from the shops was inadequately stored in bins and bags, their contents spilling out into the alleyway where the penniless had sought out anything of value and animals had sought out anything of nutritional value. The concrete surface of the alley had decayed over decades of neglect, with large puddles and deep potholes.

Harpur pulled his black bomber jacket around him and strode in long steps, his Dr Martens soles high enough to keep the majority of mud away from the leather of his shoes. Iles trod carefully, trying to avoid getting mud on his shoes. He tucked his trousers into his bright yellow socks, the vividness of his clothing clashing garishly against the monochrome of the alley.

As they came to the end of the alley, they saw a block of ten garages, five on each side. The last on the left had its old wooden doors hanging off the hinges. Harpur indicated the garage and he and Iles went over to it.

From the door they could see that the garage still operated as a drop-in centre for people needing privacy to service their essential needs: druggies needing a place to service their habit, hookers needing a place to service their clients. There were a couple of old, stained mattresses, discarded needles, second-hand condoms—the currency of a vibrant, unregulated marketplace.

Harpur enjoyed being at the scenes of incidents and crimes. He felt that he could communicate with victims and criminals, understanding more of what had happened, absorbing atmosphere and, perhaps, spotting important details. He remembered the incident report. The body had been found lying on his back, fully clothed, eyes open. There had been a syringe and needle. They had been kept as evidence, and analysis had confirmed the presence of heroin.

Harpur observed, 'Seems like quite a well-used venue.'

Iles asked, 'How were police notified?'

'Anonymous call at around ten a.m. Seems unlikely that no one saw him before then—he was cold and rigor had set in—he'd been dead for hours. As we can see, plenty of business gets transacted here.'

Harpur looked around and thought a shabby curtain moved in one of the flats overlooking the alley. He didn't want to have Iles involved in the investigation any more than was necessary and didn't feel it necessary to mention the potential for witnesses—he'd come back later. Alone.

One of the storekeepers emerged from the back of his shop. He was a striking man, tall and slim, with a more than passing resemblance to Charlton Heston. He had a scar on his jawline, red and angry although not new. He put a bin bag into a council-provided wheelie bin—a futile gesture because it would be turfed out by scavengers long before the bin men could collect.

Iles called over, 'Lovely day for it.'

'For what?'

'Appreciating the Constable-like quality Britishness of this setting—redolent of the Hay Wain? My colleague and I were just visiting the last resting place of a poor chap to see if there is anything to learn from his tragic, drug-addled ending.'

'Cops. With a new and well refined sense of sarcasm. You'll go far.'

Iles replied, 'How very astute of you. I wonder how your cop-detecting instincts have become so acute. What do you know of the death of the poor chap?'

'As you can see, this is an area that has been allowed to deteriorate—
I've written to the council and the local paper, but no one seems
interested. I found out about the death when it was reported in the
local paper.'

Iles said, 'Colin, is this anyone known to you? I can't believe he
hasn't crossed our path before.'

Harpur replied, 'No one known to me, but I haven't worked this area
of the force before. Let me introduce us. This is Superintendent Iles,
who has recently joined us, and I'm DI Harpur. We're investigating
the death that happened here a couple of weeks ago. We'd be very
grateful for any insights you could give us on this tragic event.'

'As I say, Mr Harpur, I only found out about it when I read the
papers.'

Iles said, 'I'm trying to get a feeling for the area. I wonder if we
could come into your shop for a chat about the crime challenges. As
a correspondent with the council and local paper, I can see you are
a man of rare and valuable insight.'

He considered how to refuse; they'd just walk around to the front of
the shop and walk in anyway. He smiled broadly and opened his
arms in welcome.

'Of course. What could be better? Lovely to have the opportunity to
discuss matters of concern with my local police. I'll make some tea.'

He hoped that there would be a demanding customer to drag him
away from his guests.

Inside the off-licence, Iles surveyed the scene with an approving expression.

'You have a lovely shop here. The variety of single malts and cognacs reflects well on you and your clientele, although one or two of those bottles look like they haven't moved in a while.'

'I like to offer my customers a wide range of high-quality goods.'

Iles continued, 'Yes, I can see that. Thunderbird wine is popular in any high-class establishment. I think they serve it at the Athenaeum. How long have you been here?'

'Oh, fairly recently, the ageing bottles notwithstanding. I was fortunate in a business deal and was able to fund the rent and stock. I'm doing OK, but it's not going to make me rich. I hope to be a feature of solidity and class in this part of town. I think the people around here appreciate it. It comes with the flat upstairs—not yet of the standard I would wish, and occupied by the delightful Eric, who is not currently contributing to the rent, but I feel it a duty to support those less well off than myself.'

Iles said, 'How very noble. And what kind of business deal was that?'

He replied, 'Oh, look at me neglecting my guests. Mr Iles, how do you like your tea?'

Iles said, 'Don't bother with the tea; what type of business?'

'Of course, of course, you'll need to be getting on. Lots for the police to be doing. Business… just a bit of buying and selling.'

Iles said, 'Was that scar the result of over-enthusiastic buying and selling?'

'Just an unfortunate accident involving a glass door.'

Iles continued, 'With whom do we have the pleasure of speaking?'

Ember was snookered again. He could have tried to resist telling the cops anything, but he knew that they could find out what they needed to know through the liquor licence, so he smiled broadly.

'Of course. Ralph W. Ember, at your service.'

Harpur said, 'I think we need to be back at the station. I'm sure we'll be seeing more of Mr Ember.'

'I look forward to it,' Ember lied.

Chapter 4

Harpur arrived at work early on Monday. After his first week in his 'caring' role, he had reviewed the majority of his seemingly uncontentious files and was more than slightly troubled by some of the risky cases that didn't seem to have been identified.

His predecessor had obviously been counting the days to retirement and felt no reason to be concerned. Harpur didn't have that luxury. Not only was he remarkably young in service and age to be a DI, he was also doing his rotation of roles as part of his accelerated promotion course. He couldn't afford to drop the ball. But, on the other hand, no one senior wanted to be told of a lorry-load of risk sitting in cases that had previously been classed as routine. Harpur planned to go through the files again and identify the top two or three highest-risk cases—those involving deaths with pushy families who wouldn't let an unexplained death be forgotten, or those with clear investigative failures that could easily become public.

His plans were thrown into disarray immediately. The uniform duty inspector knocked on his door.

'Colin, we've got a case that's going to need your expertise.'

Harpur sighed. 'Really? Tell me all about it.'

Inspector Mallard described an apparent suicide. A woman had been found hanging in a garage attached to a house in a well-to-do area of the city.

'The trouble is that it's Scrubby Fletcher's wife.'

Scrubby, another inspector—so called because his face was always red, as if recently scrubbed—was well known in the force. He was an ex-services man and had been in charge of cells and custody arrangements in the force for many years. Always to be found in a perfectly ironed uniform and bulled shoes, the rules and regulations of the custody environment served him well. He was popular and well regarded. Never one for spontaneity, he was reliable and well informed.

'I suppose I'd better get to the scene. The chief and the new Super will want a report.'

Harpur and Mallard went to the semi-detached house in a decent estate. Scrubby's approach to work could be seen in the house and garden as they arrived. The perfectly manicured lawn sat in front of an immaculately maintained house. All window frames looked newly painted and windows were clean. Harpur wondered what people would make of his rather more ramshackle flat.

A uniform constable stood at the end of the drive, noting details of everyone entering and leaving. The scenes-of-crime people were already there, sprinkling dust everywhere. The body had been left in situ, awaiting the expert eye of the DI—Caring.

A rope had been thrown over a roof beam. Gladys Fletcher hung there, her toes brushing the ground as the rope had stretched. A chair lay on its side. The scene of momentary violence was at odds with the perfectly organised garage: ladders mounted on hooks on the wall, two bicycles on stands, a tool cabinet with neat labels stating the contents of each drawer.

A door connected the garage to the house. He went inside and spoke to Scrubby. He was still in his uniform trousers and shirt. His face was red, as usual. He looked tired, his eyes sunken with dark bags. Night duty could be a crippler.

'I'm so sorry. Can you tell me what happened?'

Scrubby described coming home off night duty, stopping off at a supermarket and coming into the house. He had expected to find Gladys making breakfast before she left for work as a district nurse. When he couldn't find her, Scrubby had searched the house and discovered the scene. He could see she was dead and had not interfered.

'You know, we always suspect the last person to see the victim alive, and that was me—last night when I left for work—so I thought it best to leave everything as I found it. I don't want anyone imagining that I moved things to cover myself. Isn't that terrible—I've lost my wife and the first thing I'm worried about is you lot making unsupportable connections. I packed the kids off to school—they don't know yet, and I don't know how I'm going to tell them.'

In the front room, Harpur found an envelope with 'Alan Fletcher' typed on it. As it was unsealed, Harpur carefully took the letter out and read it. It was typed:

Dear Alan,

You know how difficult I have found things recently. You have been such a support. I don't feel I am worthy of you or the children.

I was thinking about my life, how I had such ambition, becoming a nurse, marrying you and having two wonderful children. But now, I'm clear that I do not deserve your love or that of Charlotte and David.

I hope I am not being selfish. I truly believe you will be better off without me.

All my love

It was ended with a handwritten 'G.'

Harpur put the letter back in the envelope and slipped it into his pocket.

He went back to speak to Scrubby.

'The note talks about things being difficult recently. Any idea what that's about?'

'Oh, you know, we had our ups and downs, a few arguments. They seem to happen more often once children come along. But there was nothing I noticed, really. I thought she was pretty happy. We loved each other but weren't in love, if you know what I mean?'

'Yes, I think I do.'

***

Back at the station, Harpur was briefing the chief and Iles. Iles was sprawled over his office chair, legs stretched out in front of him, allowing him to admire the cut of his trousers. The chief was pacing around the office.

Harpur concluded his briefing.

'It's a little too straightforward. We'll know more when we have the PM and SOCO reports.'

The chief's eyes opened very wide and his head snapped up to fix Harpur in his gaze.

'Too straightforward? What does that mean?'

'Well, only that everything is perfectly laid out, as you'd expect, and suicides are not generally like that.'

'Are you suggesting foul play—the criminal hand of another? The death of the wife of a serving police officer?'

The chief seemed to be grasping vaguely connected ideas and forming them into some kind of strategic picture. When he had put it all together, he continued:

'Oh dear, oh dear. This will reflect badly on the force—and only a couple of months after I took up my post. What will the Police Committee make of it? And what will the Home Office mandarins think? Those fuckers at *The Post* have already been stirring trouble with their focus on malicious and unfounded allegations about heavy-handedness. We need to think strategically about how to respond. Des, what's your take? You have some rather useful experience of dealing with allegations of brutality. How did that affect day-to-day issues in your last force?'

Iles stretched his arms behind his head and appeared to stifle a yawn.

'Yes, definitely useful to have experience of being subject to those allegations. I can't imagine how I managed before. Don't worry about it; there's no connection here. Our foremost investigator, DI

Harpur, is on the case. It will be difficult to connect Scrubby's wife's death to police brutality. But—'

Before Iles could finish, the chief clasped his hands together, as if trying to wring some sagacity from them.

'But I worry about people thinking this is a cover-up; that we're being far too easy on one of our own, who should be regarded as a suspect. I think you said, Colin, that he was the last to see her alive, and we all know where that leads.'

Iles said, 'That's why we point to our foremost investigator: to show how seriously we're taking it, etcetera. We need to be careful about filling in gaps that no one else has seen.'

The chief sighed. 'Des, I take your point about the link between a private matter and the force, but I think we have to have clear blue water between us and the investigation. There can be no suggestion of a cover-up, and I've got to make sure that Jeavons doesn't find a reason to get involved. I think that we'll need to get an external force to investigate. I wonder if my old force would do us a favour. I think I still have some emotional capital over there. They'd do a good job and would be discreet, leading to a clean bill of health for us.'

Iles stood up as if he'd been electrocuted.

'Forgive me for speaking candidly, but are you fucking mad? In your haste to cross the force boundary to take up your post here, did you forget about the constant sniping of those Micks about this force? Do you think they're going to forget about the Masonic influence here? Scrubby's on the square—grand pooh-bah or something—he's fully festooned in the regalia. They'll see conspiracies everywhere. Clean bill of health—in your fucking dreams.'

The chief had gone pale.

'Thank you for your admirable candour. But there doesn't seem to me to be an alternative. We could ask the Met, but frankly, I don't want them here patronising us as if we were trainee investigators. Remember how they dealt with Countryman—more than a suspicion of corruption there, but even the top man, Robert Mark, couldn't unravel it. Left him advertising tyres!'

He wandered out of Iles' office, pausing in the corridor while he decided which way to go.

Iles said, 'I find it quite hard sometimes to fathom the chief. He has, no doubt, some exceptionally useful skills, but he's also paralysed by doubts about his own competence and, in this case, the competence within the force.'

Harpur replied, 'There's another tricky issue regarding Scrubby. He's got a shotgun certificate.'

Iles said, 'That sits under my list of various responsibilities. Unless this useless shower from the other side find anything, he can keep his certificate. The impact on morale would be pretty severe—cop loses his wife in the worst of circumstances, and we compound his grief by suggesting he's a suspect, not to be trusted to carry on his pastime. Have we briefed the politicos? It's bound to get in the press, and no one likes to read about these things without having been told about it first.'

Harpur said, 'Yes, you should have a copy—it's gone to Jeavons and the Home Office.'

The following day, Iles and Harpur were speaking to Detective Superintendent Bush.

'I'm glad to be here to give some support around this sensitive matter. I will, of course, keep you fully informed about how the investigation is going.'

'We're really very grateful for all you're doing for us,' Iles declared.

Chapter 5

DC Francis Garland was talking to Harpur. Garland was tall and slim. He had the ability to make anything he wore look stylish, in contrast to Harpur's ability to make anything he wore look too small. He looked too young to be a cop, let alone someone who had spent time in uniform before moving into a detective role.

Garland said, 'Ember's an interesting character. He's got no convictions but has been perilously close to some quite tasty incidents. He was suspected of being involved in some high-value drugs trafficking that one of Tacette's team was eventually convicted of. You'll have seen the scar on his face—naturally never reported to police, but the thinking is that he upset someone criminally significant.'

Harpur remarked, 'I didn't think it was cosmetic surgery gone wrong.'

Garland continued, 'He's known by some as "Panicking Ralph"— apparently, he froze during a high-risk job. Nothing more is known about it.'

Harpur said, 'He could be someone useful to lean on—he'll still have the links with his colleagues, and him panicking under pressure could be something we could arrange. I wouldn't want him thinking that our interest and support for him was just a passing phase—he needs to know we're with him for the long term.'

Garland noted, 'He'll be thrilled.'

Harpur looked around the station yard for another pool car—he didn't want to use the Viva again in case it got noticed, or more importantly, in case its repeated visits to the crime scene drew attention to him. He found a brown Morris Marina and booked it out.

He parked a little way from the scene and walked through the wider roads of the Esplanade. The early evening trade in human flesh was picking up as the light drained away, allowing the evening to take over. As he walked through the streets, the street girls shrank back into the doorways and alleyways. Any thoughts Harpur had about being inconspicuous were banished—these people were so well practised at spotting cops, he had no chance.

As he walked on, a painfully thin woman stepped out. She puffed on the last dregs of a Number 6.

'Is that you, Mr Harpur? What drags you down to these parts?'

Denise Davies was in her mid-twenties. She was wearing a bright pink blouse, her nipples proud against the flimsy cloth, reflecting the inadequacy of her attire for the temperature. Her tight shorts emphasised the anorexic thinness of her legs. The hollow cheeks and dark bags under her eyes told Harpur that nothing had changed since the last time he had dealt with her.

'I've moved on to a new role,' he said, 'and I'm looking around the new patch. I see that things haven't changed much for you, Denise.'

'Not Denise, Mr Harpur—Desiré, like in French. It's got an accent on the second e.'

'How very grand! How is business these days?'

'It's not too bad—but your Vice Squad makes things pretty tricky sometimes. Trouble is, all the girls get caught every now and again. We end up in court, get fined, and have to work to pay off the fine, get arrested, and so it goes on. I suppose it's a bit of supply and demand—the magistrates demand money, and we supply it.'

Harpur said, 'Do you know anything about that druggy's death the other week?'

Desiré replied, 'I knew him—we called him Copsey, like he was a cop. Funny, eh? I don't suppose it's so funny now. He was a pretty heavy user, into shoplifting and burglary to finance the habit, but a nice guy. We was all surprised when he croaked—he'd been a user for years and knew his limits. But anyone can get a shit hit.'

'You haven't heard anything else about it?'

'What are you thinking? As if I could tell you anything if I knew.'

Desiré hurried off to the one working street lamp nearby.

Harpur continued to the garage. The alley was dark and seemed unoccupied. He turned on his torch and looked in the other open garages. They were similar—mattresses, discarded needles, small empty self-seal bags. He felt he was being watched and turned around quickly to check the overlooking flats. Feeble lights barely penetrated the dark but probably fulfilled fire-safety law. Just enough light was emitted to illuminate a gently swaying curtain.

Harpur climbed the metal fire-escape stairs to the first floor. He passed industrially boarded-up doors and windows—no one was going to be squatting here. The bannisters were freezing to his touch, and he tried tiptoeing, but the metal of the walkway clanged as he moved, giving plenty of notice of his imminent arrival.

He came to a flat with a door and some windows. He knocked on the door and, as he expected, there was no response. The large gap between frame and door told of years of neglect and the ravages of weather. He got out a credit card, slid it between lock and hasp, and let himself in without causing damage.

Harpur felt at home straight away. The disorder of the flat spoke to him about the occupier—it spoke of someone on the margins, scraping a living, prioritising their habit over the other essentials of life. Where did it leave Maslow and his theory of needs?

Harpur turned on his torch and started to check each room in turn. He didn't attempt to hide his presence. Whoever had been watching him would know he was there and, judging by the decrepit furniture, wasn't someone likely to invite the attention of the police.

In what was probably meant to be the main living room, Harpur found an elderly man. His clothing was elderly too and had probably fitted him some years ago, before age had robbed him of weight and muscle. He had the gaunt features of deprivation and addiction, like so many in this area of town. Grey whiskers covered his cheeks and chin. His hands were blue and veiny, caused by the cold and lack of nutrition. He stood, ready to confront, inadequately, any threat.

'Who are you? Get out—you've no right to be here.'

Harpur said, 'It's Eric, isn't it? That's an interesting view you've got of the alley. Do you see anything of interest?'

'No. And why would I tell you if I did?'

Harpur replied, 'Because if you don't want inconvenient police visits, you'll tell me all about anything interesting you've seen in that alley. I understand that life can be quite hard at the moment. And I'd be happy to pay for useful information.'

Harpur reached into his back pocket for his wallet.

Eric's cloudy pupils widened. 'Now that you mention it, I did see some activity down there on the morning that Copsey was found. There were a couple of big blokes at the garage. I didn't see them doing nothing, but they're not locals—I know the usual punters.'

Harpur asked, 'What did they look like?'

Eric said, 'They were quite well dressed—well, in that their stuff seemed to fit them quite well and didn't have holes. My eyes have gone, so I don't see very well. That's about as much as I can give you—pretty valuable, eh?'

Harpur handed over a fiver. Eric's hand took the note with a speed remarkable for someone in such an apparently rundown state.

***

He headed off to a meeting of domestic violence charities that he had agreed to attend. As he entered the meeting room at the local authority HQ, his eyes were drawn to a beautiful woman dressed in jeans and an azure-blue sweater. She had deep brown eyes and long, dark, straight hair that rested on her shoulders.

The meeting started, and Meghan Jackson introduced herself. She was working on her master's and had got a placement with a local support group.

Harpur had learned all the right language for this sort of meeting. Whilst he really was committed to getting after violent men, he didn't support the more radical agenda being spouted by the various representatives. To Harpur, it was a form of groupthink where every speaker had to be more outraged or radical than the previous one— the speeches were pointless unless they upped the anger. He also knew that his support was going to achieve little because of the lack of enthusiasm for the agenda in policing—it wasn't regarded as 'real' policing. So, he'd do what he could, knowing that gravity was against him.

As the meeting broke up, Meghan walked alongside him as he left.

'It's good for the police to be here. One day someone is going to look at the figures and find that the number of women dying at the hands of their loved ones is a fucking scandal.'

Harpur was surprised by the swearing; it looked out of place on the lips of this beautiful woman.

'Probably, but don't hold your breath.'

They walked along the high street. There were women wrapped up against the cold and the occasional beggar looking out hopefully from the doorways of closed shops. Woolworths was doing good trade, the window piled high with boxes of chocolates. The department stores had bright and aspirational front windows; well-dressed mannequins placed artistically among fantastically expensive dishwashers and washer-dryers. Garish awnings protruded over the pavement from the frontages of small businesses.

As they walked, Harpur described his work and Meghan talked about her university course. At the crossroads of the high street, Harpur went to turn right but Meghan went to turn left.

Harpur said, 'I've got to go back to the office. Do you fancy popping out for a drink tonight?'

'That sounds great.'

She gave him her telephone number, and they went off in different directions.

Harpur tried not to walk with a skip in his step, but he felt very good about himself.

Chapter 6

Barton was in full dress uniform; he was not keen on wearing it, preferring a more casual appearance, believing that this would make him more approachable—a remarkable self-deception that took little account of the rank structure in policing.

Iles said, 'My word, uniform suits you so well. You really should be seen in it more often.'

'Thank you, Des,' the chief replied. 'As you know, I seek to unfreeze the connections between command and the street.'

Harpur said, 'Do you think it's possible to undo the formality and structure of the police rank system by what you wear?' He immediately regretted patronising someone on whose patronage he relied so much.

Iles, revelling in Harpur's discomfort, added, 'That's an interesting observation, Col. I have found, through my time working with the chief, that he has a rare ability to transcend the ranks.'

Barton said, 'I'll need you two close to me at the exhibition. I'm regretting agreeing to open it—the speech will be OK, but I'll be quizzed by Jeavons and *The Post* about Scrubby. Of course, I can't say much, but that will be interpreted as stonewalling. Jeavons will then try to engineer some unpleasantness with the police committee, and *The Post* will publish a vaguely derogatory article about me. I need you two to bolster my approach—give it some depth and credibility.'

Iles said, 'We're always there to help, but I'm not sure how much depth and credibility you can get from Colin.'

They all travelled to the exhibition at the Lyndhurst Gallery in the chief's official car, a cavernous black Austin Princess.

At the gallery, Harpur met up with Meghan. He had started feeling a little out of his depth with her, almost punching above his weight. She was beautiful, and her eyes seemed to draw people into her aura, making you feel special—the focus of her attention. Today, she was dressed in a formal, long black dress. It hugged her slim figure.

Iles had met up with his long-term girlfriend, Sarah. She was closer to average height and more curvy than Meghan, without being plump—a fuller figure. She had blonde hair cropped into a bob that framed her round face. She was more casually dressed, in Levi jeans, a silk blouse, and Hermès sandals.

Meghan asked, 'How did you two meet?'

Sarah replied, 'We were both having a go at carpentry at the local college. Des is very keen on exploring things that you might not expect to be of interest to him. I think he's trying to make sure his brain doesn't ossify.'

Iles added, 'So delicately put—ossifying brain. Yes, it's true that one can become narrow-minded. Sarah was remarkably good at it. I found the constant focus on joinery a bit tiresome. And with the new challenges in the force, I've had to step away. I might have a go at welding next. I quite fancy all that heating and hitting as a way to relieve some of the pressure of work, not to mention the fitness benefits.'

The four of them began to look around the exhibition.

Iles said, 'We'd better split up—we can do more glad-handing separately.'

Iles and Sarah went off in one direction, and Harpur and Meghan went the other way.

The paintings and photographs were the products of local artists. The chief had felt it important to attend to demonstrate support for local people, and he didn't want to be thought of as a philistine.

Meghan stared at one of the paintings and moved back and forth to get different perspectives. To Harpur, the modern art piece was a blur of gaudy, uncoordinated colour. It seemed at odds with the piped, gentle prog rock of Mike Rutherford.

She said, 'I can feel the anger. Do you feel it?'

Harpur replied, 'It's certainly got some emotion.'

She laughed. 'Abstract not your thing?'

'I've definitely heard of it. Koons—is he abstract?'

'Good effort.'

As they looked at the picture, another couple joined them. The man, tall, well-built and well-dressed, spoke to Harpur.

'She has a good eye for art, you know. This captures the artist's mood, and there is a jagged depth to the colours.'

Harpur replied, 'I can just about cope with *The Scream*, but I'm afraid I just don't understand abstract.'

The man replied, 'It's not for everyone, and art is richer for there being different tastes. Wouldn't it be boring if there were only impressionists or, I suppose, abstracts? I'm keen to support our local talent.'

His partner, younger, pretty and well-dressed, was speaking to Meghan. They were earnestly pointing at the painting and were deep in conversation.

'Shall we leave the women to it? I could guide you around some of the other paintings and perhaps give you some insight. Only from my own research, of course—not because I have better taste. I always say to Mattie, "Taste is subjective. There is no such thing as bad art, only art I don't like."'

They told the women that they were moving on and that they would meet up later.

'I should introduce myself. I am Jack Lamb, local art dealer and pillar of society.'

Harpur said, 'I'm Colin Harpur, detective inspector and expected to be a pillar of society. I hope that doesn't put you off.'

Lamb's big face brightened, and he showed a full set of white teeth in a broad smile. 'Not at all. I like to help the forces of law and order from time to time, you know—contributions to force tombolas, attendance at memorial events. Oh yes, a true supporter.'

Harpur wondered how coincidental their meeting had been.

Side by side, the two of them formed a considerable barrier to anyone else wishing to view the art.

As they moved around the exhibits, Lamb said, 'Disturbing death the other day in the Esplanade—reported in the paper as an overdose. It says such terrible things about our community—there are drugs being openly dealt on our streets, and a poor man dies as a result of his habit. You note I say "as a result of his habit," not "by his habit." I know you'll pick up the nuance.'

Harpur said, 'I'm looking into that case, but I think you already knew that.'

Lamb kept his stare straight ahead at a painting.

He continued, 'It struck me as unlikely that an addict like that would overdose. They do, of course, but the report in the paper made it all seem a bit neat—addict on his own, drug paraphernalia conveniently on show, no witnesses. I wondered if there could be more to it.'

Harpur said, 'Yes, I wondered the same.'

After some moments of silence, Lamb said, 'Should we go and have a seat in the café? I think it will be quieter in there and we can contemplate the exhibition.'

At a table, Harpur cuddled a paper cup of coffee.

Lamb said, 'In my line of business, I do hear things about some unpleasant happenings. You might have guessed that I'd heard something of the death of Mr Drummond. From what I hear, it is intended to put some heat into the drugs trade.'

Harpur asked, knowing that he would not get an answer, 'Who is putting what heat onto whom?'

Lamb replied, 'Some of the paintings here are quite good. I might make a couple of offers—something local always adds to a collection and will interest my clientele. I have a living to make, after all. I'm sure we'll be in touch.'

With that, Jack Lamb walked back into the exhibition hall to join his partner.

Harpur rejoined Meghan.

'You know how I hate the way you men assume that we women want to talk to each other. As it happens, Mattie is very interesting and knows her art. She has great taste and shares her passion for art with Jack.'

On the other side of the exhibition, Iles and Sarah were looking at a black-and-white photo of a woman standing on a rock, with a turbulent sea behind her. Councillor Sylvester Jeavons joined them.

'Mr Iles, so nice to see you here. I hope you are enjoying the challenges of your new force.'

'Mr Jeavons, how nice of you to ask. It's early days, but I think it is clear that the chief has extraordinary plans for improving the force, and I am honoured to have been asked to lead implementation of the plan. The chief told me that implementation is one of his favourite words, and I was known as "Implementation Iles" at my former force.'

'All excellent to hear. I wonder whether your work will include improvement to the service given to those less fortunate than ourselves.'

Iles asked, 'That's quite a broad category of people. Do you have any particular group or groups in mind?'

Jeavons turned to face Iles. He had a full grey beard and was wearing an old suit, with shiny patches on the elbows from endless desk leaning. He had sharp, piercing eyes, giving the impression of someone who missed very little—a detail-oriented man.

'I think we can all be concerned about the use of police powers in relation to black people and the poor response to domestic violence. I think the Met has now set targets for arrests at domestic violence incidents. Is that something we should consider here?'

Iles, looking resplendent against Jeavons' shabbiness, said, 'Poor old victims won't know whether they're coming or going. Met policy has been to arrest no one for domestic violence unless the victim was close to death. Now they're arresting everyone, even if the victim doesn't want it—their heads will be in a collective spin. We'll have a look, of course, but it doesn't sound like a sensible approach to policing.'

Jeavons said, 'I see. Perhaps I could ask about a particular case—the death of the young black man, Drummond. Has that case come to your attention?'

Iles said, 'Definitely. One of our very best detectives is reviewing the case. I can't promise that there'll be arrests, but then again, we don't have evidence of an offence, and even you, in your zeal for improved services for minorities, would still expect arrests to happen only when there has been an offence.'

Sarah said, 'Inside that manicured exterior, Des is a truly compassionate man and is committed to supporting the chief in implementing his improvement plan.'

Jeavons replied, 'Lovely to see you have the support of such a lovely lady.'

Jeavons walked off to continue working the room.

The chief was standing at the lectern at one end of the exhibition, and he pinged his wine glass for attention. As silence fell, he began his speech—full of worthiness and cliché. It was warmly received and supported with occasional 'hear, hear' when he talked of support for local artists.

Iles spoke to the chief after the speech. 'Beautifully balanced as always. I've had a conversation with Jeavons. He's going to need some guiding about his thinking.'

Chapter 7

Back in south London, Else was talking to Meredith and Calvin.

Meredith said, 'We was around the area, checking to see whether the message has been received. We was looking to see if any of Loxton's people was operating off the Esplanade.'

Calvin joined in, again worried that his cruciality might be missed.

'We spotted this big bloke chatting to one of the toms. Looked like a conversation that wasn't about business, and then the Tom walked off. The bloke was big build and crammed into a cheap suit—classic Old Bill.'

Meredith continued, 'So, we follows him off. And he goes to the garage where we left Copsey. Next moment, he's off up the fire escape to the flats opposite. Quite funny watching a bloke built like a brick-shit-house trying to walk along quietly. He sounded like he was wearing tap shoes inside a fucking big bell.'

Meredith and Calvin laughed at the thought.

Else's brow was furrowed, causing her eyes to squint. 'And what happened?'

'He broke into one of the flats. Was gone for a bit and then came out and left.'

'Did he see you?' Else asked.

'Definitely not. But why was he there?' asked Calvin.

'I've told you about thinking before. If he's a cop, he's worked out that this was no overdose, and he's looking for witnesses. You two witless wonders were spotted dropping Copsey off. The cop is ahead of you.'

Calvin exclaimed, 'But no one lives in those flats. Definitely no way no one lives there.'

Else kept her voice low and measured in spite of the provocation 'Get back down there. In fact, I'm going to come with you and find out who or what is in that flat. And deal with it. We won't get seen this time.'

***

Harpur's phone rang in his flat, interrupting a daytime repeat of *Kojak*. Jack Lamb's voice burbled, 'I hope you don't mind me calling you at home. I thought the exhibition was fascinating, and I wondered if you might want to swap notes.'

Harpur replied, 'Definitely. Lots of scope for us to discuss our mutual interest. Where would be best for you?'

Lamb described some derelict pillboxes, the vestiges of the Second World War, out on the seafront, away from the tourists' cafés and shops. Half an hour later, Harpur had parked the Vauxhall Viva and was striding up the grass bank, away from the tourists' haunts and towards the place described by Lamb.

There was no cover outside the pillboxes, and the chilly, penetrating wind whistled off the sea, funneled by the estuary. Patchy, hardy grass sprouted between the dunes' sand. Harpur trod carefully, avoiding the sand as much as possible—getting it all out of his footwear later could be tricky and often futile.

Inside the concrete pillboxes were empty bottles, broken glass, graffiti and a smell of urine. It seemed to Harpur a terrible disrespect to what the concrete structures stood for—noble defence against an invading army; a single, small country gallantly standing up to a vast, unstoppable force.

No one was around that day. Harpur had put on a heavy, long coat. His hair flapped around like the strands of a mop. He pulled his hands through it in a vain attempt to restore some sort of order.

After a short while, Lamb followed the same route Harpur had taken. Lamb was wearing a long surplus woollen navy coat. His impressive frame was exaggerated by the coat—the shoulders giving an impression of squareness and the large gold buttons delivering gravitas. He had on a pair of Hunter wellies and had wisely added some sort of American navy cap, dark blue with a braid of high rank. He had pulled it firmly down to his ears to make sure the wind didn't steal it.

The two of them walked along the front, buffeted by the wind.

Lamb said, 'These were built to keep an eye out for the Germans— they were supposed to delay an invasion. I like to come here, to remind myself of the greatness of our country and to convince myself it's worth fighting for.'

Harpur replied, 'There is something majestic about their decrepitude and existence—there are no insults that can diminish them. To the end, to the end, they remain.'

'It was about the need to fight for greatness that I wanted to speak. I was pleased to hear that you are digging about relating to dearly departed Drummond. I heard that you had visited the scene and talked to some shopkeepers. You asked about who might be putting some heat into the drugs trade. I've got to be careful about my information—too much know-how from the constabulary might lead some to speculate about where their information comes from, and that could lead to danger for me.'

Harpur nodded—he had, of course, used informants before, but none who operated at the level Lamb seemed to be at.

'I wonder how you know these things—my phone number, my visits to scenes of crime, for example?'

'Friends of friends,' Lamb replied.

He went on, 'There's a London crew who want to move in here. Drummond was their way of saying that they want some specific areas for trading. Loxton sees this as a challenge, as he should. The problem for him is that this is a challenge way beyond anything he is used to. The comfortable trade here suits everyone—any unpleasantness stays within the traders, and the middle-class punters get reasonably safe and affordable products. This new lot could bring in a whole lot of disequilibrium, and that's bad for everyone.'

***

Back at the station, Harpur said, 'What if the Drummond death was an indication of something more significant?'

Iles replied, 'You've got this worked out, haven't you? You've concluded that it's either an accidental overdose or something more serious. What's that Met phrase—no-shit, Sherlock. Have you discovered anything to give your doom scenario any weight? Have you been out cultivating your contacts among the dross and dregs? You know any informants are to be a force resource, not your standing army of grifters, tipping you off every time they are worried about something that might affect their nefarious businesses. Last time I checked, you had one informant logged to you, but nothing heard from her for ages—Denise, was it?'

Harpur replied, 'If it is something more significant, we could be caught flat-footed—escalation in violence and we are not informed enough to react effectively. It could reflect badly on the force, and we know how worried the chief is about how the politicos are viewing us.'

***

Loxton was in his gold Granada with Norman Vardage and Syd Lycette. He liked this car—it reminded him of *The Sweeney*. And while they were cops, he liked the way they operated.

'Copsey was a tragic consequence of vigorous, frenetic supply and demand. But we need to be careful not to let Tacette think he can do whatever the fuck he likes without creating more unpleasantness. So, we'll burn his house—make sure no one's in. He'll know we're no soft twats, but real heavyweight businessmen to be reckoned with.'

Vardage said, 'What happens if Copsey did just die of an overdose? What if the Esplanade rumours are wrong? What if it isn't Tacette? What happens if it's someone else?'

Lycette replied, 'For fuck's sake, Norm. Have you got any more questions? Would you like a judge-led inquiry, like the look into the Brixton riots? There's areas of grey, we all recognise that. But it all adds up—the Esplanade rumours about a message. The marks on the body. Copsey's well-known expertise on dosage. Benny's given it lots of thought, and I, for one, support his deep consideration. So, let's get on and lob the brick through the window and follow it up with the bottle of petrol. Perhaps not subtle, but a beautiful efficiency, with no areas for misinterpretation.'

They drove to a street some distance from Tacette's house. Vardage and Lycette got out. It had gone dark, and they were dressed in black.

Vardage leaned into the car. 'We'll keep an eye on the house for half an hour, to make sure there isn't no one home.'

They walked the fifteen minutes to Tacette's house and secreted themselves in driveways either side so that they got the best coverage. The to-and-fro of workers coming home from work and carrying out their early evening errands with children and at takeaways had petered out. The street was quiet, lit by the orange glow of sodium lighting and the flickers of televisions.

The lights in Tacette's house were on but didn't change. There was no flickering of a TV.

After half an hour, Vardage joined Lycette. 'We're as sure as we can be that there's no one home and we don't want Tacette turning up.'

They walked over to the front gate. It was locked. There were some hedges and trees that gave them cover, and they used them to scale the fence unseen. They put down the rucksack and took out the brick they had brought along. Vardage pulled out the bottle of petrol in his gloved hands and stuffed in the rag. He shook the bottle. Vardage threw the brick at the front window. It broke with a colossal bang. They waited a few minutes to allow residents to look out of their windows and see nothing amiss. Then Lycette lit the rag with his lighter and lobbed it in through the hole.

The light from the flames danced about, casting shadows and light on the far wall. Then the flames themselves could be seen. As Lycette and Vardage left, the front window looked like a wall of flame.

***

Leo Tacette looked around his smouldering front room. The acrid smoke from the burnt carpet caught in his throat. He was wearing a decent navy-blue business suit with a black pinstripe. He liked to wear this type of clothing even at informal gatherings, to project gravitas.

That evening, he had been to church with Daphne, his intended. They had discussed arrangements for their wedding. It seemed odd to be marrying after such a long time together, but she craved the sanctity of marriage. He wondered if she had become aware of her mortality and was worrying about how she would present at the pearly gates. He was happy to keep her happy. It need not inhibit his other liaisons—marriage was just a word to him. Nothing else would change.

After the sanctity of the church, they had gone to see *Airplane*. Daphne had then left to visit her mother, a meeting Tacette was keen to be unavailable for.

He was tall and slim, and the pinstripes accentuated his elegance. He had a small moustache that he thought lent him an aura of maturity.

He was relieved to find that the fire hadn't taken hold and there was only damage to the carpet, with some minor smoke marks on the walls. All could be repaired easily enough with a new carpet, a lick of paint and a spray of air freshener. He was particularly relieved that his artwork was undamaged. This was for two reasons: firstly, the proceeds of his business had been channelled into art as a form of investment and laundering—Jack Lamb had been particularly useful in spotting up-and-coming artists who offered good returns. Secondly, had the fire been more substantial, the brigade would have sloshed water everywhere, doing more harm than the flames, and the police would also have attended, leading to awkward questions about both the art and the cause of the fire. Add to that the rumours about this new senior cop, Iles, and the whole thing could have been considerably more uncomfortable.

According to the stories, Iles had an uncanny ability to sniff out ill-gotten gains and a vicious, muscular approach to those possessing them. Tacette was keen to keep Iles and his mates at a distance.

However, there was no mistaking the smell of petrol. The fire had been deliberately set, and he needed to know why. Was this some yobs doing random damage? That seemed unlikely—they would have needed to come out armed with a bottle of petrol and just happen upon his house, then climb the locked gates before chucking a brick and the bottle through the window. No, this was much more deliberate. But who? And why?

He would put out a few feelers through his business network around the Floss estate and down the Pavillions. He'd get his boys, Lay Waste Tony and Gerald to do some asking around.

Later, Lay Waste and Gerald arrived.

Tacette said, 'We're lucky your mum's away for a few days. We need to get this place cleaned up, and I've got to know who and why.'

Lay Waste, an eighteen-year-old with long rocker's hair, wearing jeans and a white T-shirt, said, 'This is a declaration of war. We've got to be ready for some tasty conflict.'

Tacette replied, 'That's what I'm worried about. We have a lovely little set-up here. Benny's got his area, I've got mine. We've got a great arrangement about the casinos and clubs. We're both comfortable, so I don't understand what a war could be about. And I'm not keen to use words like "war." It might lead us into making bad moves. And I've heard of this new cop in town who seems to have a very nasty side to him. He might be trying to undermine our comfort.'

Lay Waste said, 'What? Are you thinking that the cops might be behind this?'

Tacette replied, 'From what I hear about this Iles bloke, nothing would surprise me—but not even he could set something like this up so quickly. He's only been here a couple of weeks. He's hardly got his feet under the table, let alone making arrangements to set the fucking table on fire. But there are others who might be well-connected enough to get it done. This guy Harpur has all sorts of contacts and isn't against some unconventional methods.'

Gerald said, 'Maybe they need some paying?'

Tacette said, 'As well as trawling the estates, give Barry Leckwith a call as well. See if anything has come across his desk at police HQ.'

***

Else, Meredith and Calvin got out of their stolen Ford Escort. It was a cold, dark, overcast evening. Drizzle hung in the air, the type of rain that wasn't teeming but seemed to get into every nook and cranny of clothing, a penetrating dampness.

Else was wearing a long black coat with Ox Blood Dr Martens.

'I'm going to sit in the car, doing my make-up. You two go out and check the area for cops on surveillance. We know their tactics – naff coloured Transit or Sherpa van with something draped over the back windows. If there's one about, it'll look too clean.'

Meredith and Calvin went in opposite directions, keeping well clear of the alleyway and the garages. After 10 minutes they met up a little way away from the alleyway entrance.

Calvin said, 'There's no one here – I've had a really good look around. Nothing that looks like an obbo van.'

Meredith said, 'Same where I looked. No cops around. Let's get Else.'

The two men wore trainers. With Else in her rubber soled boots, they were able to climb the fire escape more quietly than the heavy footed Harpur. They followed the same route as Harpur, passing the boarded-up flats, until they came across the one unboarded door of

Eric's flat. Meredith looked at the feeble Yale lock and leant heavily against it. The door gave way and they went in.

Eric was listening to his transistor radio through his earphone. Else, Meredith and Calvin moved carefully through the flat, making as little noise as they could. Eric's elderly ears, filled with the sound of his radio, didn't hear their approach. Meredith grabbed hold of Eric's arm, lifted him off his chair and pushed him against the lounge wall.

'How very lovely, don't you think Robin? A place with a lovely view and rare ambience.'

Eric stayed silent. He knew that he wasn't going to be leading this conversation.

Calvin said, 'Alfred, I think you are right. Yes, rare ambience captures it very well. How rude of us not to introduce our companion. This is Barbara.'

Turning to Eric he said, 'I don't think it would be wise to fuck us about old man, even with the rare ambience and everything. And with our lovely new companion. A bit of straight forward honesty is likely to be best. Otherwise, my friend and I can be quite unpleasant, if you catches my drift.' He slapped Eric hard across his face.

Eric's eyes watered at the sharp pain.

Else said, 'You had a visit from a cop. What did you tell him?'

Eric said, 'Where did you hear that? I've had nothing from the cops – I don't speak to cops, even if they visit. They haven't been here so nothing told to anyone. If that's all, I can forget about your entering my home and hitting me. I understand you may have been very concerned about....'

Else looked at Calvin with a resigned expression. Calvin punched Eric in the stomach. Eric doubled over and gasped for breath. Calvin brought his knee up sharply into Eric's face and blood started to pour from his nose. He swept Eric's legs from under him. Eric landed heavily and Calvin kicked him in his stomach. Eric gasped again and, winded, struggled to get any breath.

Else leaned down, speaking right into Eric's face and said, 'We feel disrespected and hurt. We're hurt that you would try to tell us lies. I know we hardly know each other, but I thought Robin here was clear about the need for openness and honesty. And look what happens when you are not open and honest.'

Eric had to decide whether to carry on with the deceit or make a rush for the truth. Either way, there was no help coming and he couldn't get away.

'Yes, you're right. I remember now. A cop did come around. He was asking about the druggy death a few weeks ago. I had nothing to tell him, so I told him nothing. So you can...'

Else gave Clavin another glance. He kicked Eric in the face, then he leant down, grabbed the neck of his shirt and dragged him up to a sitting position. 'I'm getting a little tired of these lies Eric. As Barbara was saying, we takes this as disrespectful and hurtful.'

Else said, 'I'm not sure he's quite understood the gravity of the situation. Perhaps Robin, you could explain it a bit more clearly.'

Calvin pulled a penknife from his pocket and flicked out a blade. 'Things could get very bad for you very soon.' Eric spat out the blood from his mouth and the blood from his nose continued to flow onto his clothing, forming a widening crimson stain.

Eric calculated that telling them he had seen them at the scene with Copsey and then told the cops would probably lead to his death. 'I promise you, I told him fuck all because I had nothing to tell him.'

Else said, 'That's so disappointing to hear.'

They dumped the car in a deserted car park at a local beauty spot. They put the clothes they had worn at Eric's flat on the back seat, doused them in petrol and set it all on fire.

They transferred into the Granada and began their drive back to London.

****

Ralph Ember went to check on Eric as he hadn't seen him for a few days. For the first time in his life, he called the police.

Chapter 8

'It seems there were some unexplained bruises on her body. Normally, it wouldn't be enough, but they've also had the suicide note tested by a writing expert. He says it's not likely to have been written by her—it has perfunctory, utilitarian wording, like it's a report,' Harpur ended with the thing that the chief had hoped would not happen, 'and they've arrested Scrubby.'

'There's also talk of Gladys having an affair with her dentist. According to her friends, she'd had enough of Scrubby and was about to walk out, taking the kids with her. Could be enough to be a motive. And he doesn't get on with his in-laws. They thought that Gladys was held back by him and always looked down their noses at him.'

The chief was pacing noiselessly about his office—no shoes and a deep carpet. His voice moved up through the octaves as he spoke.

'This could have ramifications. This changes everything. Jeavons will be on the blower as soon as he hears; can you make sure he hears it from us? It's bad enough having the policing lead smelling blood, quite literally, but if he feels we're not being up front with him, it could get very nasty. He's already talking to the Home Office about falling standards… I've only been here a month. What does he expect?'

He looked around the room. Iles was, as usual, immaculately dressed in a tailored suit. He was wearing another pair of expensive shoes. Harpur was, as usual, barely contained by his suit.

Harpur wasn't sure what expression would convey the sentiment that the chief couldn't be blamed for failure so early in his tenure. He opted for nodding but was aware that he could be interpreted as agreeing that more could be expected in a month, so he added, 'Unreasonable,' but he felt that was insufficient endorsement of the chief's position, but he'd missed his moment.

Iles said, 'It's a tricky one. I expect Scrubby will hold his story. Swift will be feeling some of the same pressure that we do, but from a different direction. He can't be seen to be going soft on us, as if he would. And the complaints people are looking over one of his shoulders, with the Home Office looking over the other. So, on this one, we hold firm. Wouldn't you agree, Mr Davies-Hywel?'

Davies-Hywel was, as usual, in uniform. His shirt had lost the vividness of new and now leaned more towards off-white or light magnolia. 'It is a difficult situation. Should we suspend him? It's not a great look, having someone suspected of murder working in the force.'

The chief gulped.

'All in good time, Aled. I think we need to see what happens with him. But we cannot be seen to be acting slowly or indecisively. I hope I'm clear.'

Iles was in Harpur's office and asked, 'When do you think we would ever want to be seen to be as slow or indecisive? It's one of those bullshit phrases that we seem to like so much in policing— "reassurance patrols" that actually remind people that something awful has happened, "facilitate legitimate protest" that means allowing the great unwashed to fuck up everyone's daily routine. I don't object to using the phrases; the public and politicians like to hear them. But I do object to us believing they mean anything.'

Harpur wasn't sure if he was supposed to answer and decided to move the conversation on. 'What about his shotgun licence?'

Iles said, 'I've escalated that particular hot potato to the ACC. We could find ourselves in a rather difficult dilemma. We don't want to suspend Scrubby if he isn't charged, and, frankly, from what I know, they won't have enough to charge him. So, we'll probably need to move him into a job counting paper clips. That makes it a bit harder to take his certificate back, not only is it the certificate, but we have to go round with his mates on the firearms unit to seize his guns and ammo. I can imagine that going down like a bucket of cold sick. Anyway, this is all now in the land of the stratospheric brains of our ACPO man, Davies-Hywel.'

Harpur changed the subject. 'We had a call from the esteemed Ralph W. Ember this morning. He discovered his tenant dead in his flat. I'm on my way down there now. It's not my investigation, the main office people will take it on, but I thought we might like the opportunity to revisit Mr Ember—see if he has any information he'd like to pass on to us.'

Iles smiled. 'Sounds like a fine idea.'

***

Harpur wasn't trying to hide his visit to the alley, so he took a CID Allegro in beige. It was close to the top of the range and had a big but gutless engine connected to an inadequate three-speed automatic gearbox. The suspension made the car rock back and forth like a liner in a heavy sea, whilst the engine gasped and wheezed as it generated barely enough power to move, and the gearbox shifted clunkily back and forth as it desperately sought enough torque.

Ember was in his shop when Harpur and Iles walked in. 'I've already told your colleagues all I know. I hadn't heard from Eric for a day or so, and I went up to check on him. He was dead. Looked to me like he'd been stabbed, but I am, of course, no expert.'

Iles said, 'Is there anything else you might want to tell us, your new friends from the police, that you haven't mentioned to our colleagues—anything that you thought too trivial for them but, on reflection, might be of value? Anything that you might consider your friends, the police might find out anyway and might be offended not to have been told by you. You know, things that might lead to significant enquiries into the source of funds for a shop, for instance?'

Ember said, 'That's the thing about Eric—kept himself to himself, had very little to do with anyone, but didn't miss much going on around here. He did mention having an unexpected visit a few days ago, someone interested in the Drummond death.' Ember looked at Harpur.

Harpur said, 'Yes, I did have a look around in the evening a few days ago, seeing what could be seen in different types of light. I ran into Eric and we had a nice chat. Nothing useful forthcoming, unfortunately.'

Iles responded, 'Thank you for that. That's exactly the sort of thing I had in mind. Of course, I already knew about that because Col had briefed me.'

In the car on the way back, Iles said, 'Is this the type of backhand activity I can expect from you? Going off on your own flights of fancy?'

Harpur said, 'I didn't think the Foreshaw investigation would fall within your remit.'

Iles said, 'Everything that suggests shit for the chief or for the force is in my remit. Do you think your intervention with your size elevens has resulted in Eric's demise?'

Harpur said, 'It had occurred to me. Obviously, I was very careful to check I wasn't being watched and took an undercover car—the usual precautions.'

'It seems like the usual precautions weren't enough. And that tells us an awful lot about Drummond's death. I think we might need to visit some of the other players in town.'

***

Harpur and Iles stood at Benny Loxton's front door. Iles was wearing uniform. Paul Esposito, known as Pablo the Pocket, opened the door, and Iles walked in without being invited.

'Where's Benny?' Iles demanded.

Pablo said, 'He's in the downstairs khazi. He'll join us in a moment, I'm sure.' Iles nodded his head to a door off the small hall. Pablo raised his eyebrows in assent.

Iles went over and pulled the door open, destroying the lock in the process. Loxton was sitting on the toilet, trousers and pants around his ankles.

Iles said, 'What a joy to see you, Benny, and looking so well. Detective Inspector Harpur here has told me all about you, and I can see he has failed to reflect your true grandeur in his description. But by the smell, I think I can definitely advise a review of your diet.'

Loxton replied, 'Do you have a warrant for this intrusion?'

Iles exclaimed, 'Intrusion? Surely not. This is nothing more than a welfare visit. There have been some unpleasant happenings, and we are concerned about your health. We feel it our duty to make sure our foremost businessmen are in the pink, and I can see you are definitely pink.'

Loxton said, 'Do you think you could piss off whilst I pull my trousers up and wipe my arse, but not in that order?'

In Loxton's crowded front room, Iles and Harpur sat on a leather-covered Chesterfield settee with Loxton and Pablo on armchairs. Loxton looked at Iles. 'So, why are you here?'

Iles said, 'As I mentioned, there has been some unpleasantness—the deaths of Drummond and Eric Foreshaw. Or maybe you hadn't heard?'

Loxton said, 'According to the papers, Drummond was an overdose and neither he nor Foreshaw had anything to do with me, so I really don't understand why you are here.'

Iles smiled broadly. 'We were meant to believe that Drummond, also known as Copsey, was an overdose. But we have an ace detective on the job, someone with outstanding investigative ability but somewhat less developed artistic taste, as you can tell from the clothes. He has discovered that Drummond was probably murdered.

Foreshaw was probably a witness and has been silenced. As Drummond was one of your dealers, we wondered whether you might be worried about your own safety?'

Loxton replied, 'How very thoughtful of you. I have no idea what you mean by suggesting that I had any connection to Drummond. That could be libellous, but I'll let it pass because you are obviously struggling to show your effectiveness as a police force, and your judgment might be affected by stress. I'm feeling perfectly safe, or at least I was until you arrived. I'd be pleased if you'd leave me alone now. I don't need your help.'

Iles and Harpur drove towards Leo Tacette's place. Iles said, 'He seemed pretty confident.'

Harpur said, 'Yes, but he doesn't know where the threat is coming from.' Iles looked at Harpur. Harpur kept his eyes on the road as he drove. 'What have you heard?'

Harpur replied, 'Nothing too specific, just that this might be a set of out-of-towners.'

'Who is giving you unspecific information such as this?'

'Yes, possibly a group trying to muscle in on the trade here, but nothing specific.'

Leo Tacette answered his door and invited the two cops inside.

'How lovely to have a visit from the local police. What can I get you to drink—tea, coffee? You'll not be drinking alcohol, of course. All of that type of behaviour is ancient history.'

Iles replied, 'Thanks. You can forget the refreshments and irony. We're visiting our high-profile businessmen to make sure they are all bright-eyed and bushy-tailed. You'll have heard of a couple of incidents connected to the drugs trade—deaths, Leo, of a dealer and a possible witness. We want to offer our services to you to make sure that you remain safe and well.'

Tacette sat on a brightly coloured settee. He had managed to combine bright colours and strong geometric designs without them clashing dreadfully. Tacette said, 'That's an interesting opening. Of course, I have no idea about the drugs trade, so I fear you have made a wasted journey.'

Iles sniffed the air. 'Maybe we're too late? Have you had a visit from some unfriendly people? The smoke smell is quite discernible in spite of your game efforts to cover it with an air freshener. And the signs of hasty redecorating suggest that something significant has happened.'

Tacette replied, 'One of the kids messing about with fire. Set a rug on fire. Nothing for the police to worry about.'

Harpur said, 'I see. You might be interested to know that our information is that the threat is from outside the area. You would do well to think about that. Once you have, you know where to find us. Superintendent Iles can be incredibly supportive of our local people. But he can also be quite unsupportive if he feels that local people are not participating properly in community life.'

Tacette said, 'I'd heard.'

Chapter 9

The chief said, 'Well, I suppose that is good news. It means they don't think they've got enough to convict him. But it does cause us a problem… Where do you employ in a police force someone who is a suspect for murder?'

Harpur added his usual gritty caution. 'Not enough to convict him yet. And him being out and about does present us with other difficulties, such as the safety of the dentist.'

The chief's smile disintegrated and was replaced by a furrowed brow and a wave of his hand, as if trying to bat away the inconveniently obvious.

Sounding irritated, the chief said, 'Yes, yes, of course. And we can't tell the dentist about the risk either, so no chance for alarms and the like, unless we can concoct some other type of threat. Could he have a particularly malevolent patient angry about a crown?'

Harpur replied, 'Not that I know of. We've got some coverage of him with a light surveillance team. I don't want to put a full team out because the intel is quite weak and, if we put a team there, we can't put it somewhere else.'

The ACC interjected, 'We can leave the brains branch to look after the risks, thanks to DI Harpur. But we'll have to get Scrubby back to work. He can't be involved in anything operational—wouldn't do to have a murder suspect offering policing service on our behalf. He has to be miles away from any of the top team—there could be terrible rumours of collusion, access to privileged information, not to mention the opportunity for him to be turning your desk over, looking for clues, whilst you are out of the office. I'm not sure having a murder suspect in Personnel is a fantastic idea either. Perhaps he could be in charge of some traffic prosecutions?'

The chief was looking much better. The good news about Scrubby had enabled some colour to return to his face. He was in uniform again and had, again, dispensed with shoes. He felt this mixture of formality and informality struck the right balance between gravitas and approachability.

'Let's find a job somewhere, preferably something that doesn't look too much like a sinecure. Then there's the shotgun stuff. I'll leave that decision to you, Aled.'

The ACC replied, 'Thank you.'

Iles sat in Harpur's small office. Iles was in uniform today. He had had the whole lot tailored to fit. Whilst practically every other member of policing looked like their uniforms were either too big, small, long or short, Iles's was immaculate, his shirt sparklingly white and the red inserts on his superintendent crowns vivid against the pure white background.

'That's a tricky decision for the ACC,' said Harpur.

'Why do you think I involved him?' asked Iles. 'If he decides to suspend his shotgun licence, it will cause uproar. He's a bloke who has lost his wife, has been arrested and released. From their perspective, he's an innocent man and, more importantly, he's one of our innocent men. But, leave him with it, then the ACC's at the mercy of the Micks deciding whether or not to charge him at some stage in the future. If they do, the ACC will be in deep shit for letting a suspected murderer keep the means to commit murder. In an ideal world, the investigation ends and Scrubby is in the clear. But no one gets any plaudits from that outcome. Everything is on the risk side with almost no reward.'

Harpur said, 'I've got some friends over there. I could see if I could find something out—whether they've got anything else or whether they are close to calling an end to it.'

Iles said, 'It would be useful to know, but I wouldn't feel obliged to let the ACC know. I think he could be someone who thrives on stress.'

***

Tacette phoned Loxton. 'You daft cunt. You thought it was me who did Copsey? We need to talk. Meet me at our favourite place when we were at school.'

Loxton replied, 'I know where you mean.'

Later, Tacette was striding across the St Mary school field, down the muddy bank on the far side and across an open area to a small bridge over a stream. He could have come a shorter way, using a car and walking a small distance down a footpath, but he considered that Loxton had already tried to torch his house and didn't feel inclined to give him another opportunity for ill-placed revenge.

Trudging across open land like this gave him no cover, but also meant that should Loxton want to kill him, he'd have to have people following him—difficult over open land. And, if the cops had a tap on his or Loxton's phone, they'd have to follow him or Loxton to the rendezvous; more difficult across open ground.

73

Tacette was confident he hadn't been followed. He went and stood in a small wooded area, away from the bridge. He would be able to see Loxton arrive and make sure he was alone. It was dark, and the local yobs had broken all but one of the lights that helped guide walkers with their dogs. Clouds drifted across the moon, intermittently blotting out any dim natural light.

Loxton was also worried about being followed either by Tacette's people or by the cops. He also took an elaborate route and secreted himself away from the bridge. At the appointed hour, he moved slowly towards the bridge. Tacette saw him and also moved carefully towards the bridge.

Loxton indicated that they should walk along the footpath, away from the road. Tacette followed, looking all around him to see if there were any of Loxton's people hiding in the foliage. The path followed the course of a stream on the right and opened into a more open area, away from trees, with houses backing onto the grassy area.

After a couple of minutes of this checking and following, Tacette felt this open area was a secure place and caught up with Loxton.

'Benny, long time since our school days, eh?'

'Let's get to business, Leo. Very wise not to talk too much on an open line. Who knows who might be listening… I see that you don't quite trust me, with that piece not very well hidden under your coat.'

Tacette said, 'I don't expect that you came here without taking some precautions. You think I did Copsey? And then Foreshaw? You'd be a bit daft to come to meet me unprepared. You look a bit more bulky. Is that body armour?'

Loxton said, 'So it wasn't you who did Copsey? I put some ears out around the Esplanade, and the word around there is that someone is putting the heat on me to stop me expanding my operation beyond the Esplanade. Who else would want to do that?'

Tacette said, 'I had a visit from the cops yesterday. The new bloke, Iles, came along with that detective with a face like a failed boxer. He said the pressure was coming from out of town.'

Loxton said, 'They visited me too. Why do you think they would give us this information? Perhaps they're looking for a cut, maybe a bit of police protection? They didn't seem to be talking as if that's what they wanted. You know, I'd expect a bit more respect and some coded messaging. Instead, Iles marched into the bog whilst I was sitting down and was less than decorous.'

Tacette said, 'I wondered that too. Maybe they're worried about some turf war that might make them look even more incompetent than they already do? You know, *The Post* has been showing up the failings for years now, and the chief has hardly had a good introduction, has he? What with one of his own nicked for murder and two other murders, all within a couple of weeks of his arrival. Hardly the new broom sweeping it all clean.'

'So, how do we find out what they want? I've got someone who's quite well connected at police HQ. I could see if he's heard anything.'

Tacette nodded. 'Sounds like a good idea. And let's leave the Copsey and Foreshaw business alone for now. As the Godfather might say, "it's only business"—but not for them, obviously. And if you ever have the idea of attacking me or my family again, you had better be fucking sure that you've got the need to do so. Otherwise,

I shall be more than slightly pissed off. If we are going to have a war, let's make sure it's for a good reason. And as you know, rather like our business, the war goes on and on and on. We only ever win battles. Rather like that useless lot of fuckers up at police HQ, their war never ends, they can never win it. They only want to win a few battles and keep those they lose to a minimum. They don't really give a shit about the community. That's just the flim-flam du jour. They want to look effective and do as little as possible to achieve it. Maybe we can help them achieve their aims. How very public-spirited of us!'

The two of them stopped, faced each other and shook hands. They departed in different directions.

***

Harpur's phone rang in his flat. Meghan rolled over and groaned.

'Is it usual to get disturbed like this on the weekend?'

'I've spoken to a few villains and asked them to keep their offending to office hours. I have had limited success.'

He'd had one of the new angular phones fitted. The lurid orange added to the impression that he was speaking into a piece of cheese. It was 8.30 on a Saturday morning, a strange time to get calls from anyone.

If it were work-related, he'd have been called earlier, when the first CID teams had got in. None of his friends or family would call at this hour unless it was a dire emergency.

Jack Lamb's beefy tones cleared up any mystery.

'I wondered if you fancied a walk by the sea today?'

Harpur said, 'Yes, nice day for it.' He got out of bed, pulled back the curtains and saw steady drizzle. 'Well, niceish.'

Harpur was dressed warmer than the last time he had been on the promontory meeting Jack Lamb. He counted himself a fast learner. He wore a bobble hat, a leftover from a school skiing trip. It didn't convey the impression of importance, but it did stop his hair dancing around like an uncontrolled marionette.

Although the wind was not as strong, it had been cold for days, and the grassy hollows seemed to swallow the cold, releasing it only when there was someone there to appreciate it. Lamb turned up, as usual, from a different direction to Harpur. He was looking magnificent in a long leather coat topped with a blue beret.

'I hear that you've been seeing our commercial leaders. They are uninformed about the direction of danger.'

Harpur replied, 'Yes, they seemed genuinely surprised when we suggested the out-of-town dimension. There was definitely a sense that there had been some unpleasantness.'

Lamb changed direction abruptly and said, 'I was at a very interesting exhibition in London earlier this week. Some quite interesting stuff. I bought a couple of pieces; you never know how careers can turn out.'

Harpur asked, 'Whose? Yours or theirs?'

Lamb replied, 'I heard some interesting discussions about a brother-and-sister team who might be looking to branch out their business into a new area. I wondered if you might want to have a conversation with the Met's intelligence people about someone called Else.'

Harpur replied, 'It's a bit vague. Is there any more?'

Lamb said, 'Don't be obtuse. There's loads you already know. Join the dots.'

'Good point.'

***

The following day, Harpur walked into the church. There were plenty of people at the front, but a sparse population in the pews. It had been a standard Anglican church, but congregations had fallen and it had been revived by the local evangelicals. There was a choir, mainly comprising middle-aged black women. There were a few younger members and a couple of white faces.

Copsey's coffin rested on trestles at the front.

Harpur sat in the second row. Sitting further back would have looked very odd and a cliché of what cops do at the funerals of those who have met a violent end.

The choir struck up with excellent, uplifting music. They moved energetically to the music, many with their eyes closed, rapt by the tune and words.

Pastor Anstruther began his address. He wore none of the usual dress cues of a man of the cloth. He was a middle-aged black man wearing black trousers and a white shirt. He spoke well of the momentary time of life on Earth and the glory of life ever after.

After the service, Harpur went to speak to the Pastor. 'Mr Harpur, I was hoping I'd see you. I have heard good things about you from some people who have not received the kind of service we might have hoped for from the police. I know that Paul's father will appreciate you attending.'

Anstruther led Harpur over to Copsey's father and did the introductions. As was so often the case, relatives of the deceased looked tired and tired of life.

Harpur said, 'Mr Drummond, I'm so sorry for your loss.'

Drummond replied, 'Thank you for that. Will anybody care about him? I assume that you being here suggests that you are not convinced by the overdose story.'

Harpur said, 'The overdose bit is definitely true. The issue is whether he did it alone. As you know, the people who are likely to know about events are not always forthcoming. The post-mortem was not terribly helpful in uncovering the moments before Paul's death. I will do all I can to get to the bottom of it, but, at the moment, all we have is an overdose and a few vague indicators of external intervention. I tell you this because I want you to know that Paul's death is being investigated, but that you should not get your hopes up about someone being prosecuted.'

Drummond said, 'All I want is justice for Paul, whatever that might be. And I can't be too critical of you. Where was I in his moment of need?'

The Pastor put his arm around Drummond's shoulder. There was a loud sob, and Drummond's whole body heaved and shook as he sobbed.

Anstruther said, 'Sometimes, those who need the most help are the ones least able to receive it. He is with God now.'

Anstruther shook Harpur's hand. 'That was a nice touch. Let him know you care, but manage expectations. Most people can live with honest, care-driven efforts that may not deliver what they hope for. What is "justice" in this case? I think it has to be the best police work, with whatever outcome that leads to. But remember, lots of people are watching and trust arrives on foot but leaves on horseback.'

***

Later, Harpur and Iles were in the function room of the HQ bar. The décor reflected an earlier era, with dark wood panelling, seats upholstered in dowdy colours and a lino floor to resist staining. PC Harry Gittens was retiring after thirty-five years, mostly spent as part of the firearms team. Harpur disliked these events. Wives and partners came along to lend a sense of family to a job that was very good at keeping families at arm's length. There was a superficiality that Harpur found hard to stomach. Early on, there would be forced bonhomie, when senior people circulated pretending to be interested in the lives of their subordinates and overly enthusiastic laughter in response to feeble senior-officer jokes. These first couple of hours were generally just about tolerable, although the speeches were rarely worth the candle. After that, booze tended to make the subordinates quite candid and senior people needed to be very careful not to be present when the candour turned to rancour. Those who got to be the most senior had a sixth sense that told them when to be absent. Harpur wondered whether he had that, but was sure that Iles definitely did.

A chief superintendent gave the leaving speech and droned on about how the job had changed from when he'd joined in the fifties, how there was a greater need for community involvement in policing. It was a lesson in policing buzzword bingo. It ended with the presentation of a card filled with witty, half-witty and the occasional sincere comment, and a model of a police firearms officer mounted on a plinth.

Iles was circulating the room, pressing the flesh with some people he knew and others he didn't. He seemed to be genuinely enjoying the event, but that was likely to be his natural acting ability.

Sarah had come along, looking effortlessly gorgeous. She was wearing jeans that wrapped themselves around her, accentuating the curves of her buttocks. Her simple blouse rested on her breasts, the sheer material shimmering on every curve. She was deep in conversation with Francis Garland. Garland was making heroic efforts to keep his eyes concentrated on Sarah's face.

Meghan had also turned up to bolster the impression of a force that appreciated the family. She was wearing looser clothing, hoping to conceal her changing body shape.

Iles and Harpur ended up at the same end of the room. 'What a splendid event. I feel that moments like this reflect the sentiments of the chief. A need for our community to thrive so that we can serve all of our other communities. We need inner strength to be able to project strength outwardly. I think that is the sort of talk that he would want to hear. In nurturing our community, I don't think it would be too destructive to ask Garland to keep his fucking lascivious eyes off my lady friend. Gorgeous as she is, and utterly committed to me, I still feel that Garland's scarcely disguised priapism is not really in the spirit of the policing community.'

Harpur replied, 'Yes, Sarah is looking lovely this evening. Did you get any thoughts from the firearms people about Scrubby?'

Iles said, 'I did do some careful exploration of issues and, as I thought, their view is that there are definite competitive overtones from our Mick investigators and that over-reaction to the investigation might not be well received here. I'll feed it back to Davies-Hywel in due course. I think he'll appreciate some more complicating insight. It is, of course, quite unhelpful that Scrubby is Senior Warden for the same Lodge as the majority of the firearms team. Davies-Hywel isn't on the square, but my information is that a number of other senior people in the force are. I'm sure the Lodge connections will have no bearing on the ACC's decision-making.'

'Do I detect some swelling around Meghan's middle? Or has she just put on a bit of weight?'

Harpur looked for a non-committal answer but could only come up with, 'Yes, she looks lovely, as usual.'

Chapter 10

Harpur looked at the intel report from the Met. Lamb had been right, making a few connections with the information he already had meant the Met were able to give him some useful intelligence. Even so, he had the feeling that the Met had done their usual trick of providing only the most obvious details, leaving out almost anything of real use.

Confidential – Police Eyes Only. Not for further dissemination without the authority of the author.

Intelligence Report for DI Harpur

Nominals Identified:

Daryl Justice PHILIPSON

Elspeth Marie PHILIPSON

Intelligence Held:

Nominals known for organised street-level dealing in and around Peckham. The source of their supply is unknown. They are viewed as tier-three nominals and, therefore, not a priority for targeting.

The Met holds a significant number of intelligence reports, some including a range of other nominals who may or may not be part of the PHILIPSON organisation, and, therefore, these details have been withheld. Should the requesting force have specific requests regarding associates, supported by evidence/intelligence, further intelligence research could be undertaken.

Latest reports, obtained from tasked intelligence sources, suggest that the PHILIPSONs may be exploring opportunities to expand their business.

Ends

***

Harpur marvelled at the portentous way in which the bleedin' obvious was delivered— *'may be exploring opportunities to expand their business.'* Which drug dealers weren't seeking to expand their businesses?

Anyway, the report provided nothing new except to confirm Lamb's information. Harpur would have to find a way to pass the intelligence to the Foreshaw team, but in a way that didn't suggest he had inside information and did not provoke further enquiries at the Met—too much interest in the Philipsons might pique the curiosity of senior people there, and the bigger the group of people aware of external interest, the greater the chance of leaks. Whilst there had been high-profile efforts to tackle corruption in the Met, Harpur wasn't entirely confident that it had all been driven out.

He was sensitive to Iles's observation about how his contact with Foreshaw had caused his demise. He didn't want to cause any more deaths, at least not of people who'd already had enough bad luck. And the chief would be deeply unhappy should there be further violence in his force area.

Harpur was sitting on the edge of a desk in the chief officers' typing pool; he and Iles were waiting to get in to see Davies-Hywel to update him on the discussions at Gittens's leaving do.

Harpur said to Iles, 'I got some interesting intel from the Met regarding the Philipsons.'

Iles raised his eyebrows.

Later, in Harpur's office, Iles asked, 'What are you up to?'

Harpur replied, 'It would be tragic if there were more deaths related to the drugs trade. It would be even more tragic if any of that unpleasantness happened in this force area. And I think we'd all be truly upset if there was an ongoing conflict about trading here.'

Iles replied, 'I see. Your view is that we're in danger of getting caught in the middle of a conflict we can't control, so let's have the conflict away from here?'

'So very succinct,' Harpur replied.

***

Loxton was speaking to Barry Leckwith. They were standing next to each other in a department store, apparently looking at leather wallets. Their conversation was conducted without them looking at each other. Loxton preferred populated places for meetings with Leckwith. He felt that meeting in dreary back alleys was the stuff of 1970s American detective TV shows.

Leckwith was a portly detective sergeant. He was wearing a crumpled corduroy jacket, paired with well-worn trousers that still had the flares of the recently passed glam-rock phase.

Leckwith said, 'Harpur talked about the Philipsons. I did some checks. Nothing came up on our systems, but we're not connected to any intelligence systems outside the force.'

Loxton replied, 'Thanks. That's extremely useful. Don't do anything more now. Any more digging will draw attention to our interest, and you're no use to us if anyone suspects you of being our man at HQ. There's no chance he was setting you up?'

Leckwith replied, 'Definitely not. He was in the typing pool, and I don't think he even noticed me at the photocopier. It was just luck I was there, and I only heard a fragment.'

Loxton replied, 'This is what we keep you on the roll for. Subtle, careful and useful. Yes, I think these three words sum up your contribution.'

***

Loxton was wearing some well-worn jeans; he liked to wear high-quality but threadbare clothing, aiming for smart-casual but more on the casual side. His T-shirt was tie-dyed and worn under a formal white shirt with large collars. He had a long denim coat with a faux sheepskin lining. He'd had his hair done recently—fair, collar-length and intended to look as if spontaneously styled, but it had actually taken some considerable effort and time.

Tacette was the same age but reflected his view of his trade in his clothing—a sharp suit. He was beginning to show the signs of age, with wrinkles around his eyes and touches of grey in the hair around his ears. He had his hair cut every two weeks with the same short back and sides.

Loxton started the conversation with his news from Leckwith.

'How should we handle this? I've heard of the Philipson lot, but I thought they were similar to us—local, small-deal dealers. It's a big step for them to step out of their area and take on outfits they can hardly know. It really fucking annoys me—the cheeky fuckers just think they can walk in here and frighten us off.'

Tacette replied, 'Maybe they think they are dealing with one outfit and that they can outmuscle you? I'm not suggesting that they could do that, only what they're thinking. How sure are you about Leckwith? He's not exactly the sharpest pencil in the box, and that Harpur is a fucking sly devil—and Iles seems capable of any sort of caper. We need to be pretty sure before we go off causing conflict with out-of-towners.'

Loxton said, 'It's occurred to me that Harpur's up to something. But Leckwith was pretty sure that Harpur hadn't seen him and that it was completely coincidental that he was there at all. Sometimes you got to trust your narks.'

Tacette rubbed his jaw and said, 'I'd like to be sure. You got any links in London? I haven't.'

Loxton shook his head. 'How about I push a dealer into a new area? We could put a couple of our people on protection duties.'

Tacette nodded. 'Going fishing, eh? It'll have to be one of yours. Paynter? He's young and maybe fancies the opportunities of a new area? Perhaps somewhere with a few pubs and bars? That new development by the docks?'

Loxton replied, 'Yes, I've got a few of the premises on my books—door staff to give the protection they need and to turn a blind eye to sniffing in the bogs.'

***

Justin Paynter was happy to look at the possibilities for extending trade into the new Grant's Hill development. Nice middle-class housing estate, with what the brochures called *an amenities and connections area*; there was the bus station, some decent shops, a Wimpy, a curry house and a Chinese restaurant. There was a large pub that had been purpose-built. It had two bars, one with lots of carpets, decent seats and tables. It was intended to attract middle-class people from the middle-class estate.

The bar at the back had a lino floor and unthrowably heavy furniture covered in hard-wearing leatherette; there was nothing absorbent in this part of the pub. There were bouncers on the doors on Fridays and Saturdays. It got very busy on these days as people bussed in from the rest of the city and availed themselves of the booze- and food-focused micro-economy to be found here. At kicking-out time, the majority decanted to Bumpers, the nightclub in the basement of the casino, with some going into the casino, seeking to win back the costs of the night.

At the end of the night, drunken couples would fall into the taxis queuing at the rank. The council did a good job of washing down the pavements early on the following mornings so that the rubbish and vomit were removed in time for the daytime business to commence.

Paynter felt at home. He was a croupier in the casino, *Les Croupiers*. He only had shifts in the early hours of Saturday and Sunday mornings, helping the clientele to be parted from their money. He was in his early twenties and had loved gambling from the first time he had done any betting. He and a group from school had been bunking off lessons and ended up at a friend's house, where they played poker for halfpennies. He worked out pretty early on that he was good at taking money off his credulous friends.

When he officially left school, he got a job at the casino. With that job came a salary and some small tips, but also a pretty hefty drug habit. He had been pleased to be able to mix business and pleasure, sniffing his gear on the weekends, in his breaks at the casino, and dealing for the rest of the week.

Loxton had always been pretty good with him, allowing him to make whatever profit he could so long as Loxton got his cut. There were lots of opportunities for getting supplies from other places or trying to talk down his profit levels to reduce his payments to Loxton. He had not done so because he knew that the local market was controlled by a small number of bigger operators. If he pissed off one, the opportunities for hiring by another one of the big players were quite small.

And, anyway, Paynter knew he was a good card dealer and that there would soon be opportunities abroad, where the tips would be bigger.

His long hair fell onto the shoulders of his leather jacket. He wore his smart trousers—bouncers could be funny about jeans, and it would be deeply irritating if trading time was lost because he couldn't get into the pub or club. Even though Loxton had guaranteed that door staff would look after him, he couldn't be sure that would extend to dropping the dress code.

***

Dawn Lincoln had left the police after ten years. She felt that she was talented and had a good policing head on her shoulders. Her supervisors and managers kept rejecting her applications for promotion, making different demands on her each time—get experience of this, work in that team and so on. Eventually, she worked out that your face had to fit.

As a woman, she was aware she was always starting at least half a pace behind her male colleagues, but she felt she could easily bridge that gap. But the gap wasn't half a step; it was more like ten.

She left and created her own private investigator business. It wasn't like television; she didn't drive around in flash cars or investigate anything interesting. She did lots of following of misbehaving husbands. It wasn't glamorous, but it paid the bills, and she was in charge of her own destiny.

This commission was a little off the beaten track; it was more like a counter-surveillance operation. She'd done that as part of her police training. Women were useful for surveillance and low-level undercover work, but only because the men needed a female to be the love interest; she had only ever been allowed to be the support to the main player.

Because she was dealing with a mark and then looking for people who might also be looking at the mark, she had decided it was a two-person job. In the police, a job like this would have taken ten people, but the pay for her work didn't stretch to that, and she'd called an old colleague, Dan Crowstone. He'd done his thirty and retired. He was getting on a bit, in his mid-fifties. And he might stand out among the young people of Grant's Hill nightlife. But he was reliable, had been a surveillance officer, and Dawn got on with him.

Dawn wore no make-up and dressed in a dowdy-coloured, shapeless jumper over jeans. Dan wore chinos and a business shirt.

As Paynter worked his way through the various bars and pubs, Dawn and Dan swapped over, one following into the premises and the other keeping an eye on exits. Their job was not to follow Paynter but to see if he was being followed.

They watched as Paynter moved through the heaving masses of Friday-night revelry. As was to be expected, he made frequent trips to the toilets followed by a series of punters.

At the Fisherman's Arms, Dan followed Paynter, with Dawn marking the exits as best she could. The front bar was packed with younger clientele, and Paynter was in his element, moving effortlessly from one group of potential customers to another. Having worked the room, he moved into the lounge bar at the back of the pub. There was a more genteel crowd in here, mostly sitting in decent-quality chairs in a setting conceived by a professional pub outfitter. Everything was perfectly coordinated and hard-wearing.

Dan followed and went to the bar. He ordered a pint of beer and went and sat at an empty table in the bay window to the side of the bar. Paynter walked through to the toilets and then returned shortly after and hung around at the bar, not ordering anything but looking around to see if there were any likely customers.

Dan noticed two men sitting at a table who seemed to be interested in Paynter. The one nodded his head very slightly in the direction of Paynter, and the other looked over. Paynter, noticing their interest, went over to their table. There was a short conversation, and Paynter left the pub quickly.

Dan didn't want to leave straight away because he would show out. He took a few deep glugs from his pint and then left by the door into the car park. Paynter had gone, and Dan could see Dawn moving down the street. He set off after her, moving quickly without running. He caught her and said, 'I think I've seen the tails. We need to get back to the pub.'

This time, Dawn went into the pub. She went straight through to the toilet and then left. She saw Meredith and Calvin sitting at the table. She met up with Dan and sent him to get their car.

After half an hour, Meredith and Calvin walked into the car park of the Fisherman's Arms. They got into their beige Ford Escort and drove off. Dawn and Dan followed. They hung back, allowing one or two cars to come between them and the Escort. But they knew that it wouldn't be long before they were spotted. They wanted to see whether they were local or out-of-towners. Meredith and Calvin drove onto the main road east out of town. Dawn and Dan peeled off.

Dawn reported her news to Loxton.

'That's why we hire someone as reliable and talented as you, in spite of your previous career! This is real good info. And you're sure you weren't spotted?'

'I can't say we weren't spotted. There was no indication that they had spotted us—no late manoeuvres, speeding and slowing down or circling. And I think we left them soon enough, even if they had suspicions. Will you want me to do any follow-up? If so, it might be better for me to bring in another associate. But you'll know that, however careful, it's hard to do good, unobserved surveillance without a full team, and a full team costs.'

Loxton paused and looked across his lawn, which had been lightly dusted with snow overnight.

'Not at the moment.' He handed over an envelope containing some banknotes. Dawn counted them, said thank you and left.

***

Sarah was in her bed, lying next to Garland.

'I think that I do love Des. He's witty, clever and good-looking in an odd sort of way.'

Garland was facing her, looking deep into her eyes.

'He certainly has something about him. There's a real sense of presence and danger.'

'But I like being with you too. I think it's a problem I have. Even though I'm happy and contented, I feel the need to find something more. Does that make me odd?'

'I don't know. I suppose we all feel the grass might be greener somewhere else. I'm just happy that you wanted to find out something more about me.'

Sarah turned over and lay on her back. She looked at the ceiling.

'You know he'll find out. He has a sixth sense. He can just spot when something isn't quite right.'

'That could make things quite tricky for me,' Garland observed.

***

Barry Leckwith said, 'It'll be a bullshit address. I can do some checks if you want, but I don't think it will get you anywhere. The only thing I think you can take as real is that the car comes from South London. I took the liberty of talking to a mate of mine in the Met. He said that one of the blokes you described sounds like one of the Philipsons' gang, Gentle Julian Meredith—you'll appreciate the irony of "Gentle." He's got a fair bit of form for violence, usually after he's had a skinful, when he seems to become easily excited. Lots of stuff with women and lots of stuff that hasn't got to court. He's not someone to introduce to your mother. And, because he's with the Old Bill down there so much, his address is pretty certain.'

Leckwith handed over a handwritten note with an address in SW9.

…

'No, it wasn't an official informant, just someone I overheard at the pub, talking about someone called Philipson who was doing some dealing around The Esplanade. I'd never heard the name, so I thought I'd just do some checking to make sure it was legitimate. I wouldn't want to be passing on any old rumours I'd heard in the pub.'

DI Evans replied 'That's very thoughtful of you Barry. Can you draft it up into a proper intelligence report and then we can put it on the system?'

'Yes, of course. I was a bit concerned that my doing some checks might cause some concern should there be any events connected to the trade in The Esplanade. I thought it best to make full disclosure to the intelligence team and make it all official.'

Chapter 11

Iles liked patrolling with the street teams. He despised the way senior officers felt it was their duty to 'do visibility' – patrol with the street teams but do only the minimum to demonstrate their support, avoiding any involvement that might mean contact with the public in conflict situations.

Iles was happy to put on his tailored uniform and join the teams as they responded to the various calls for assistance. He enjoyed the visceral, uncontrolled nature of street policing.

He was even happier if he worked with a young, attractive female.

WPC Benning was his working partner for the Friday evening shift. He attended the team briefing; all of those coming on duty flustered around him, showing excessive deference, getting him cups of tea, booking out his radio, and making sure the panda car was clean.

'Just give us the same calls as you; I like to keep my hand in.'

Benning and Iles walked out to the pale blue Allegro.

Benning said, 'You'll have to drive, sir. I can't drive.'

She was in her early twenties, with clear skin, no makeup, and a neat bob haircut, so she didn't need to tie it up under her female officer's white hat. She was pretty, with well-defined cheekbones and nose, and deep blue eyes. The skirt she wore didn't show off her figure, but it couldn't disguise a slim, well-proportioned body. She wore her uniform jacket, which afforded a similar sense of shapelessness but also did not hide her shapeliness.

They spent the first couple of hours dealing with calls left over from previous shifts. The light had dribbled away with the office workers, and the gaudy colours of the night were shining brightly when Iles drove down towards Grant's Hill.

He and Benning parked the panda in a side street and got out.

'I like to be in and amongst the nightlife. It's when I feel truly alive. I feel like I can commune with them; it's what they called me in my former force, "Communing Des." It's almost as if "communing" is my middle name; by the way, it isn't.'

Benning looked at him with a smile on her face. 'Let's go do some communing!'

They walked along the main drag, looking into the packed pubs, seeking signs of trouble. All seemed high-spirited but jovial. The streets had the usual mix of stag and hen parties, some making a beeline for the two cops for some drink-infused conversation. Iles and Benning chatted with the various groups.

Iles pulled Benning away from one group into a shop doorway.

'I know that face.'

On the other side of the road, Dawn Lincoln was fully concentrated on being unobtrusive. She stopped outside the Fisherman's Arms and spoke to Dan. Dan went into the pub.

Iles said, 'I wonder what she's doing here. I know her from my old force; she left last year.'

Benning and Iles moved back to a side street and watched. They saw Dawn and Dan leave the pub car park in a car, apparently following a Ford Escort.

Checks on registration numbers revealed that Dawn's car was registered in her old force area. The Escort was registered in South London.

At the end of the shift, Iles said, 'That was most enjoyable. Perhaps we could do it again one day?'

Benning smiled and went into the women's changing room.

***

Iles decided to drop in on Sarah. He was in his pale blue BMW 2002 Tii. He felt that he should have a car that fitted his current status, but also his future status.

He hadn't called Sarah, but he felt their relationship was going well and that they were getting closer. He didn't feel it necessary to announce a visit in such a close and trusting relationship.

As he drove towards her flat, he caught a glimpse of the tall, fair head of Garland as he walked erectly along the pavement.

Iles didn't stop but carried on and parked outside the front of Sarah's flat. Her flat was part of a Victorian house. She had the ground floor. The main door was an imposing wooden structure with stained-glass insets. It was bigger than the doors on the new builds. There were two bells, and Iles pressed Sarah's. She appeared at the door almost straight away and looked surprised to see him.

'Not interrupting anything, I hope. I've just finished a shift with the street team and need to spend some time with beauty and intelligence.'

'Of course,' she replied. 'Come in.'

Iles inhaled deeply as if trying to vacuum away the residue of a previous occupant.

Everything in her flat betrayed someone with excellent taste; modern art prints in perfect harmony of colour and design, complementing the high-ceilinged grandeur of the building. Large leather furniture suited her front room, and the wallpaper looked expensive and expertly applied. Yes, Iles knew why he loved her so much.

Sarah said, 'I'm just changing the bedclothes. Give me a moment.'

Iles said, 'Don't hurry for me. Strange time to be changing bedclothes.'

Sarah shouted from her bedroom, 'Just fancied a change of sheets; you know how lovely it is to get into new cotton.'

She walked back in. 'There, it's done. Are you staying? It would be lovely if you would.'

Iles was in two minds. Should he leave and allow himself to feel defeated by Garland, or should he stay and assert himself with her?

'Yes, I'll stay, if that's all right. I need the embrace of a warm, beautiful woman.'

'I'll go make myself warmer in the shower. Shall I get you a drink, or can you help yourself?'

Iles poured himself two fingers of scotch. Sarah soon joined him and poured herself a glass of red wine.

Later, in bed, Iles said, 'Are you wearing new perfume? I thought I detected something different when I arrived.'

Sarah said, 'Oh yes, I'm trying something a little heavier. Seems to better reflect the heavy winter atmosphere. You know, something light in spring and something heavier for the rest of the year.'

Iles said, 'It's a little too masculine for my taste. You do know how much I love you?'

'No,' she said, 'tell me.'

'Beauty and body are pretty good. But I love your discernment and, how should I put it, an almost bohemian spirit; the constant fight I feel you're having with conformity. The need to be constantly seeking the new and exciting.'

'You understand me so well. That's why I love you, too.'

'It's just that I'd like the bohemianism to be concentrated on me.'

Sarah looked into his face, but he displayed no sign of irony.

Chapter 12

The chief was pacing noiselessly again, which seemed to emphasise his impotence.

'They're going to arrest him again. They even had the audacity — or is the word "temerity"? I don't know, but they asked me... yes, me... they asked me for a statement confirming the measures I had taken to limit his role and influence in the force. A thinly disguised suggestion that we've been protecting Scrubby – I mean, Inspector Fletcher – because of his Masonic links. I can scarcely bring myself to respond to such a slight. Not only is this a slur on me personally, but also on the force and the august leadership we have in this room.'

He looked around the room, from Iles to Davies-Hywel to Harpur. Iles nodded in affirmation, and the other two nodded their support in turn, as if taking part in some weak form of coordinated dance.

Having found his tone of righteous indignation, he continued, 'I was at the chiefs' council last week with Jon. He sounded very supportive, talking about the tricky start, the pressure from our local politicians, and the Home Secretary's interest. You'd have thought he would be supportive of me after the time I served as his deputy. But it's clear he's only interested in his own future, making it look like he's getting a grip on our failings. All in the hope of command at a bigger force and a gong. I can't believe how naïve I've been to expect him to show any sort of understanding or support. Des, I remember well how clear you were about all this, and I must say that your judgement has turned out to be accurate. Jon and his shower of God-fearing Catholics are only in this for themselves. We're going to have to look after ourselves. Aled, we need some decisive action now. We cannot be even suspected of protecting our own, as if we ever would.'

Having unburdened himself, the chief seemed to relax and sat down.

Iles said, 'I don't think that we could or should have done anything differently in handling Scrubby. You delegated the decisions to a command-level officer, and you needed to remain distanced from the decision-making in case you have a role in any discipline proceedings. You are, after all, the discipline authority in the force. If I may say, I think you're being a bit hard on yourself.'

'Des, I'm grateful for those observations and your support.'

Turning to the ACC, the chief continued, 'Inspector Fletcher has been told to report to one of their police stations with his solicitor. I suspect that they have some new evidence. Have any of you heard anything?'

Harpur volunteered his information. 'My contact in the force told me that they were looking at the ink on the letter. Apparently, it can be quite specific, with different compositions of colours. It's possible that they've had some developments there. That, alongside the questionable writing style, might be enough for them to charge him.'

The ACC said, 'I think this is the trigger moment, if you'll forgive the unfortunate metaphor, for us to seize his certificates and weapons. If the firearms team get upset, we'll have to explain it and hope they see reason. Des, as you've been involved in this from the start, I wonder if you want to deal with it.'

Iles remained seated and said, 'I'd love to, but I'm out of force for the next couple of days; I'm having to tie up the final details relating to the complaints matters from my old force. There's nothing controversial, but they've asked me to be available for two days. I'm keen to get that matter resolved; it's one less thing for the chief to worry about.'

The chief said, 'Aled, I think it makes sense for you to be personally leading this difficult piece of work. Dealing with the firearms team and Inspector Fletcher's colleagues is going to take some deft and subtle handling.'

***

Later, Harpur and Iles were in the canteen. It was just after 4 p.m., so all of the office staff had either gone home or were preparing to go. The shift officers would not be in for their meals until later. They had the canteen to themselves. They sat in uncomfortable moulded plastic chairs at a Formica-topped table standing on vinyl tiles and sipped at strong, stewed tea.

The noticeboards contained vital information about the Federation and support services. They had gone brown at the edges, betraying how long they had been there, unloved and unconsulted.

Iles wondered aloud, 'How does anyone drink this? It must be bad for you. Anyway, I think I dodged a tricky one there. It's what they get paid the big bucks for.'

The ACC wandered into the canteen.

'Out of force, eh? A convenient moment to be away.'

Iles replied, 'That unfortunate matter… I think that's what you called it: is close to resolution. And I'd prefer that it's finished as soon as possible. When do you think you'll go over to Scrubby's place? I don't suppose you'll want to do it while he's away, if that can be avoided.'

The ACC scratched his chin. 'Good point. That would look bad: forcing entry into a colleague's house, and we'd need a warrant. I'll hold on until we know what happens at his return visit. If they charge him, they'll keep him in custody, and we can seize it all at our leisure. If they don't, we can seize it all when he gets home.'

***

The chief looked tired. His skin seemed to be dragging down his face like a blancmange-coloured glacier.

'This goes from bad to worse. They've charged Inspector Fletcher with the murder of his wife. As you suspected, Col, they found the pigments in the ink on the paper to match a pen in his possession— a police-issue pen, if you please. I don't know who to be most disappointed with, Fletcher or that investigating officer Swift; he's given us no advance information. He is, of course, acting in accordance with Jon's instructions. It all seems so petty. We were close colleagues when I was in that force, but that counts for nothing.'

He continued, 'There's a horrible irony that could get played out in the papers about how a police officer uses both his knowledge and tools of the trade to commit the most heinous crime; pen mightier than the sword and all that. Have either of you got anything positive to tell me about the other investigations? I know these things can take time, but I'd like to be able to tell Jeavons and the Home Office people that progress is being made.'

Harpur said, 'We've got some leads on some out-of-towners. But it's not enough to start briefing politicians about yet; we don't want to set ourselves up to fail.'

Iles said, 'I had a bit of luck the other day; managed to spot a former colleague doing a bit of surveillance around Grant's Hill. Could be linked to our investigations. I need to triangulate this with anything Col has discovered from his exceptionally opaque sources. It's not for discussion here yet because we haven't put the pieces together, but I do feel you can strike an optimistic tone with Jeavons and the colourless desk dwellers of St James's Park. Their character reflects the appalling blandness of that Home Office building next to that beautiful park.'

***

Later, they sat in the HQ bar with Garland.

Iles said, 'A piece of luck seeing Dawn Lincoln like that; good street policing uncovers a good lead. Completely unlike your disgusting and unauthorised chicanery with grasses and other low-lifes. The car she was following is registered to some non-existent place in south London.'

Garland said, 'Makes it a bit difficult? How do we get after them? Presumably, we don't want to involve the Met.'

Harpur said, 'I don't think the chief wants anyone thinking we can't handle this ourselves, and he also doesn't want the patronising tones of the Met elite. We need to think of other options.'

Iles said, 'Talking of other options, I'd just like to be clear that my girlfriend is not available to all the hoi polloi of this force.'

Harpur could see Iles's eyes narrow and the tendons in his jaw tighten. Stress red crept up his neck like a cartoon thermometer, and sure enough, Iles blew like a cartoon thermometer.

Jabbing his finger at Garland, the pitch of his voice high and loud, Iles declared, 'If you think people like you can have dalliances with the beloved of your superiors, you've made a very serious error of judgement. The lack of loyalty is not something that sits well with being a member of the police force.'

Spittle flew from his mouth as the volume of his delivery increased. Garland shifted back in his seat.

'People have crossed me before. They don't do it twice.'

Iles got up, patted down his clothing, dabbed his mouth with his handkerchief, and walked off.

Harpur said, 'I'd heard he has the potential to go off like a firework. Not sure it's sensible to be too close to the ignition twice.'

'Thanks for the advice.'

Chapter 13

Tacette was wearing another pinstriped suit. Loxton had put on a proper shirt to reflect the gravity of the meeting.

'As I said on the phone, something very significant has come to light. The team I put on Paynter came up trumps. So now we know who we're fighting, we can decide how we want to do it. My team and me were wondering whether we have a common enemy? And we was wondering whether we might want some extra help?'

Tacette nodded. 'This sounds exactly like the right approach.'

***

The chief was in full pacing mode.

'I know I left the decision-making to you, Aled, and as Des pointed out, that was entirely appropriate because of the potential for my involvement as the ultimate discipline authority in the force. But I think things have changed now. I don't wish to replace your judgement with mine. I have a command team, and I expect them to command. But I would encourage some thought about whether the situation has changed sufficiently to cause a change of mind.'

Davies-Hywel replied, 'I think that the decision about suspending is more straightforward now, if pointless.'

The chief stopped pacing and turned to the ACC, standing with his arms outstretched as if appealing to a referee.

'It's not pointless because of the message it sends; we take decisive action when the evidence supports it and the needs of the community dictate it. It also plays well to the various political interests; it tells them we've got a grip. So, Inspector Fletcher is to be suspended because he's been charged with his wife's murder. As he's in custody, as you suggested, Aled, it doesn't make a whole lot of difference in practical terms, but it does add to the impression of a force seeking to deal with some difficult issues. That sounds like the bottleless language of a schoolteacher; the force wouldn't exist if it weren't for its people. I have to show I've got a grip; I have to show that I'm dealing with the difficult issues. Of course, there is the follow-on decision regarding his guns and certificate. I think that decision is similarly easy now, but I'll leave it in your hands.'

Davies-Hywel was dressed to leave the station, which was notable in itself. He had his tunic on, with the various bits of silver embellishment that were part of a senior officer's benefits. His cap was pristine, having rarely encountered the atmosphere. He pulled on his brown gloves.

Inspector O'Reilly was in plain clothes. 'I thought we should keep this low-key.'

He was joined by PC Matthew Carson, an ex-military man.

'I've asked Matt to join us just in case the seizure gets tricky. I had to deal with a chap who'd taped a shotgun to his leg so he could commit suicide by operating the trigger with his toe. It was an absolute nightmare because of how he'd jammed himself, and Matt was the person I called to help so that we didn't put another hole in his head as we tried to unstick it.'

They got into the senior officers' unmarked beige Allegro and wallowed and pitched their way to Scrubby's house. Davies-Hywel kept taking the warrant out of his pocket, re-reading it, folding it, and putting it back.

O'Reilly said, 'This shouldn't be a problem. We've got the enforcer in the back if there's no one at home, and, if necessary, we can prise the gun safe off the wall and get into it back at the nick.'

Davies-Hywel wasn't thinking about the practicalities. He was considering whether he'd made enough notes about his decision-making. He felt the chief's concern about delays in taking action. The ACC thought it had all been justifiable at the times decisions were made. But that wouldn't help when he needed the chief's support for the next rank. If the chief felt he'd been indecisive, that could be the end of his career. He could be stuck in this backwater for years, with that malign spirit Iles nipping at his ankles, trying to force him out so that he could take his post.

Well, Iles could fuck right off; the ACC had made the right decisions at the right time. It was a skill to avoid making decisions until they needed to be made, and his assiduous attention to detail and evidence would stand him in good stead. He had almost completely convinced himself of it by the time they reached Scrubby's tidy semi-detached house.

They knocked and rang at the front door. A neighbour came over and said, 'Yes, we saw him earlier. He came in and went out shortly after, carrying a bag.'

The ACC went pale.

'Get the enforcer now.'

O'Reilly and Carson went to the boot of the Allegro and returned with the heavy, solid metal door ram. Carson swung it a few times against the front door and then handed it to O'Reilly, who had another couple of goes.

In the end, the locks surrendered, and the door bounced open. The three cops went in and started to search for the gun safe. It didn't take long for O'Reilly to call from the garage.

'Guv'nor, you need to see this.'

The ACC hurried through and saw the gun safe, firmly attached to the wall with a solid frame and door. It would have been an excellent and secure set-up, as required by Scrubby's shotgun licence conditions. Unfortunately, all security was undone by the open door and the missing shotgun and ammunition.

The ACC said, 'Carson, go to the car. Circulate Scrubby as missing. Don't mention the shotguns, just that he's missing and we're concerned about his welfare. I don't want every cop in the force on the phone to the papers telling them we've got an armed, unhinged cop on the loose. And how the fuck is he on the loose?'

The ACC used the house phone to call the chief.

***

Back at the station, the chief called in Harpur, Iles, and the ACC. The chief was in plain clothes… some good-quality trousers and a work shirt, but no tie. He had kicked off his black slip-ons and was back, noiselessly pacing his office.

'We were notified earlier this morning by fax. By bloody fax! It sat on the station officer's fax machine for hours until the late turn came in and saw it. He made a late application for bail. Swift and his team were caught off balance and didn't do a very good job of objecting. The judge seems to have formed the view that the evidence is weak and that, as an upstanding member of the force, he could be released on bail. I mean, after all, he's only charged with killing one person, so his previous good character should be taken into account.'

The ACC had never heard the chief being sarcastic and bitter like this.

'Where do we think he's gone, and why has he taken his guns?'

Harpur said, 'The superintendent and I had a discussion earlier. I didn't know much about his relationship with his wife, but I did hear that things were a little fractious between him and his in-laws. As you know, we've got a team on the dentist and they've been updated. We may need to formally brief him if we don't get our hands on Scrubby soon. I've been on to Scrubby's solicitor to find out the address of his in-laws, and they wouldn't tell me anything because of client confidentiality. I've got DC Garland on the phone with Swift's team to see if they've got any addresses. Next thing will be to search his house; bound to be an address book by the phone.'

The ACC fidgeted in his chair.

'Have you something to add, Aled?'

'There is an address book. I saw it when I phoned you.'

Iles said, 'This has become an acute tactical matter, possibly best suited to the skills of Colin and me here. With your permission, chief, we'll go off and make the tactical arrangements: brief the firearms team, get a briefing done for Jeavons and Home Office, identify potential points of risk, etcetera.'

'Thank you, Des, that's a great help. It would be tremendously useful if you could get Scrubby under control and get his guns back. This could get very ugly.'

***

Harpur and Iles sat around the table in Scrubby's dining room. Detective Superintendent Swift had joined them, as had Inspector O'Reilly. The force duty inspector had also turned up.

Iles stood, resplendent in uniform.

'I'll run you through the briefing. Scrubby is missing with his shotgun, and we fear for the safety of his in-laws and Gladys's love interest. We've got the dentist under obs, so our priority is the in-laws.'

He sat down.

Harpur said, 'Mick, can you get a firearms team straight over to the in-laws' address in Woodlands Drive? I'll try to phone them to warn them of your attendance. It's a blues and twos job.'

O'Reilly went to the hall and phoned the firearms base. He then left to join his team. Harpur picked up the phone and dialled the number from the address book. The phone rang and rang, then went onto an answerphone. Harpur left a message.

Harpur and Iles drove as fast as they could to Woodlands Drive. As they drove, the firearms team provided updates on the radio.

'Set up; cover front and back. Team at door and ready to go.'

'No answer at door. Instructions, please.'

O'Reilly replied, 'Breach.'

'We're in. No response to challenge. Starting search to contact.'

'Three bodies. Looks like shotgun wounds.'

***

Harpur and Iles arrived and walked into the back room of Scrubby's parents-in-law. An elderly-looking man sat in an armchair. He had a large wound in his chest. Pieces of tendon and muscle hung out of him, and the last drops of blood dripped into his lap. His head had fallen forward. The radio was on, and *The Archers* were discussing another rural crisis.

The door into the garden was open, and a bone-shaking cold wind passed through the room, stealing all vestiges of heat. On the patio, just beyond the door, was a female body. She had a hole in her back. Her woollen cardigan was matted with blood. Her head was turned to her left, and her eyes were open.

On the floor in the room lay Scrubby. He had a large hole on the underside of his chin. His head had swollen almost comically because there had been no exit for the shot.

Iles said, 'The chief was right. This is ugly.'

Chapter 14

The chief had his kitchen cabinet back together again.

'Well, this could scarcely have gone worse. I have been summoned
– yes, I think the word is 'summoned' – to see the Home Secretary.
I received a call from the permanent secretary. He said the Home
Secretary was concerned to ensure that I have all the support I need
to deal with this challenging situation. "Challenging"—apparently
the new word to describe catastrophe. It's supposed to make me feel
as though it's something that's part and parcel of the job—a
challenge that anyone in my position might encounter.

'I didn't feel I needed to ask whether there was any other chief who
had one of his own killing their wife and parents-in-law and then
himself. I think I might be offered the help of that prize set of shiny-
arse wallahs at the Inspectorate. Just the sort of help we need;
meetings, community involvement, and unmatched acuity in
hindsight.

'And what's worse: they've invited Jeavons. Can you believe it? I'm
going to have to spend several hours travelling with him on the way
to London. Any suggestions about points for conversation?'

Iles, wearing shocking pink socks, said, 'I suppose there might be
an opportunity to head off any criticism from him; any support
would be good. Frankly, though, the Home Sec won't pay much
attention to that jumped-up little prick. He'll only be interested in
the operational stuff, and that's your domain. I wouldn't tell Jeavons
much about the operational details; he'll want to show himself as
being in the know and controlling things here, so the less he knows,
the better. You can leave him flannelling about his constitutional

position in representing the people around here. The usual guff that the Home Sec will have heard a thousand times from people who think they're running things but aren't.'

The chief said, 'Thanks, Des; useful thoughts as always. Is there anything I can tell them about the other two matters?'

'We're making progress, and we expect some significant developments quite soon,' said Iles, enigmatically.

***

Tacette, Loxton, and Ember were sitting in Loxton's front room.

Ember exclaimed, 'What taste you have, Benny. You've turned a standard room into something grand and elegant.'

Tacette, in a pinstripe as usual, perched on the edge of an armchair. Ember leaned back into the corner of a Chesterfield. He found that they looked comfortable but rarely were; certainly not for sitting. The curves of the back weren't very soft, making it hard to snuggle into the leather.

He was dressed casually, with jeans and a navy blazer over a multi-coloured rugby top; could have been Harlequins; neither Loxton nor Tacette knew nor cared.

Loxton was wearing trousers and a shirt, open at the neck, with a curl of chest hair poking out like the top of a poodle's head.

'There's a bit of a problem, and we wants to sort it out. Could be advantageous to all of us if we forms a little alliance. Sure, it's got relevance now, but it could be relevant in the future too.'

Ember replied, 'Benny, I'm always interested in creating alliances that can promote the image of the town and improve the quality of life. We don't want all of that ghost town stuff being sung here!'

Loxton was playing some early Beatles on his reel-to-reel tape.

Ember said, 'Fine system you have there. Beatles never my thing. More into the Stones, and even they feel a bit dated now, what with punks and romantics all over the place, some looking like tramps and the others like spivs.'

Tacette interrupted, 'Yeah, all very nice. But let's get onto the alliance discussion. We knows you had a bit of luck with a big deal; nice little business you got out of it. But you ain't making enough to retire on, are you? Benny and I are doing OK with our businesses, but we've had some interlopers; that's a good word for them. Money-grabbing bastards is another. We need to deal with them, and then we can have a nice, stable dealing arrangement.

'I knows you'll understand the importance of stability for dealing, what with your previous work. We thinks there's big opportunities to expand the business. Benny and me, we goes back a long way and can play nice when we have to. These out-of-town twats will bugger everything up, so we're seeking to create a nice, strong, local union to repel all invaders. Benny and I can provide the muscle, and we felt that you could provide the community gravitas… someone who'd be able to draw in some legitimate support. You know, get the journos on side, influence councillors, and do some general arse-licking.

'And we might struggle with getting cash into banks, all nice and squeaky clean.'

Ember thought he could feel his scar starting to open up. This often happened at times of stress. It was as if the stitches had come undone and the blood would start flowing again, and the white of the fatty layers were laid bare again. He put his hand on his chin to make sure all was well there. But this was only one sign of panic. He started to sweat. Fortunately, he had kept his jacket on, and so the dark patches under his arms and down the middle of his back didn't show.

Loxton said, 'You seem like the right sort of upstanding person who could help us with cash flow. Those letters to the paper, your little business right in the shit end of town, all with the intention of promoting our little homestead, improve things for everyone. Very public-spirited and a perfect cover for cleaning some cash as well as creating the right ambience for high-quality crawling.'

Ember leaned back into the unreceptive Chesterfield. He wanted to transmit a sense of calm and control, which was a considerable distance from how he actually felt. The last thing in the world he needed was an alliance with these two low-level drug dealers. He'd already had enough of the maniacal Iles and did not wish to give him any reason for further visits. Of course, it was Ember's apparent sparkly cleanness that attracted Loxton and Tacette, but that made Iles and his sidekick suspicious. More cash flowing through his business would only draw more unwelcome attention.

Hoping to erect some insurmountable obstacles, Ember said, 'This sounds like a fantastic proposition. I'm excited to hear about the details, how it would work, etcetera.'

Loxton said, 'It's pretty straightforward. You put our money through your business and pays it back to us through various innocent-looking business arrangements—cleaning, building works, you know the sort of thing. In the evenings, you attend worthy events, exhibitions, charity concerts, you know the type of thing. And you speaks to all the right people, getting them all sympathetic to your points of view. Then, when we need their help with, say, some licensing or planning decisions, you've got the inside track. All above board and kosher... well, nearly.'

'It sounds fantastic. How do you think I can cover the amount of money you would be talking about through a small off-licence? The tax man would be suspicious for starters.'

Tacette said, 'That's the beauty, and Benny didn't mention it because he was all excited because this is such a perfect arrangement. We reckon you sell your off-licence and get another, bigger venture. You can choose whatever you like. Car rental's big; maybe a chain of book shops; anything legit that can turn over a fair bit of cash, cash being the most important bit. We was talking about music earlier, record shops are doing well. Something that might have a few tax breaks could be good as well, maybe a building needing repair. I don't know why I'm telling you this. You'll be way ahead of me, thinking through the possibilities. You raising obstacles is just your way of thinking it through.'

Ember tried to sound excited but worried that he might have sounded more scared. 'You've obviously had the time to talk this through. I need a little time to think about the details, the practicalities.'

Loxton said, 'Leo and I have thought through a few practicalities ourselves.' He put a stack of notes on the table in the middle of the room. Tacette did the same.

'You see, we could imagine that you wasn't going to be particularly keen unless we could demonstrate very clearly the advantages. We wasn't thinking you'd clean our money for nothing. We thought a fifteen per cent cut would be fair; you're not taking the bodily injury risks that Leo and I take every day. But you would be taking tax risks as well as giving the cops a reason to be interested in you. There's twenty grand there; it's a tidy sum. Could buy you a decent house around here. Think of it as a down payment, to help you think through the practicalities.'

Ember's eyes widened. It was true that the cash did make the arrangement far more attractive. 'Give me a couple of days to think about it. As I said, I need to consider a few practicalities.' He picked up the piles of cash and stuffed them into the pockets of his jacket. Tacette and Loxton looked on, smiling.

'We're sure you'll make the right choices,' said Tacette.

Chapter 15

At Else's address, Meredith and Calvin were reporting back on their observations at the Fisherman's Arms.

'He was definitely dealing. Hadn't seen him in there before. He could've been a lone operator, but that would be dead risky for him. He came over to us and asked us if we needed anything. I think he got the message from us pretty sharpish because he fucked off quickly. I reckon he was one of Loxton's boys.'

Calvin, again fearing his role might be overlooked, added, 'So we followed him off a bit and then came straight back here to let you know.'

Else took a long draw on her Sobrani and blew out a narrow stream of smoke through pursed lips.

'We need some presence on the ground. I can't exercise the control that I need at this distance. When we move in there, I'm going to need some feet on the ground, people who know the area. You two need to get a place down there. Keep an eye on developments, spot people who might be useful for business, cops who might be helpful, that sort of thing. I think I'll come with you to make sure the job gets done properly.'

Meredith said, 'Fucking hell! Who wants to live in that stagnant backwater? Not me!'

'I'm thinking a couple of months max. Enough time for Daryl and me to get things set up, find the right people here to place down there for a spell. And having a place already set up for our people to move in and out could be very helpful.'

***

Else had found a room in a bed and breakfast hotel just off the Esplanade and paid in cash for one night. She had sent the two men to search the area for promising places from where to run their operations.

Calvin and Meredith paced up and down the streets just off the Esplanade. They were in prime student territory.

Meredith observed, 'There'll be lots of places for rent, and the constant turnover of residents won't draw attention.'

It was bright with early spring sun.

Calvin said, 'Not the best time for finding student housing.'

Meredith said, 'There'll be a few places that have been abandoned by drop-outs and some that weren't rented out at all. And we'll be looking at the top end; we need somewhere pretty big, with lots of rooms.'

After looking in several estate agents and tramping up and down streets, they'd got a few options, and so they started visiting and making calls.

Meredith was in a phone box speaking to someone on a number they'd seen on a sign outside a decent-sized Victorian house.

'Cummon, it's just around the corner. Could be good. It's the upper floor and there's a kitchen, bathroom, and four bedrooms. I don't suppose it'll be like Mayfair, but we got to be prepared to slum it a bit for a while.'

St Edward's Terrace was full of large Victorian houses that had been converted into students' digs. In between, where bombs had dropped in the war, some newer blocks of flats had been built. The road was quite wide and accommodated lines of cars parked on both sides of the road. The cars described the affluence of the area—rusty Minis, Hillman Imps, and Austin 1100s, the cheap runabouts of the students and the down-at-heel permanent residents.

Meredith and Calvin knocked at the impressive front door at number five. Michael Poole answered. 'Let me show you around.'

The first floor was accessed through a door off the hall that led straight onto the stairs. The previously ornate and substantial staircase had been replaced by something much narrower and steeper, enclosed by the external wall on one side and a plasterboard wall on the other. A thirty-watt bulb shed feeble illumination onto a grey nylon carpet. The walls were a light shade of magnolia and showed the signs of many trips up and downstairs by people carrying large boxes and bags, with scrapes and chunks exposing pink plasterboard.

'Classy,' said Meredith.

Poole spoke with a cultured accent and carefully constructed his sentences. 'What were you expecting? These are student digs; they live here for a year. Generally, not the type of arrangement that encourages loving respect for the property in which they stay. But you have the opportunity to upgrade and put your own character into it. I'd encourage that and would celebrate your individuality being displayed in your decorations.'

Calvin couldn't contain a snigger. 'Oh yes, you can count on individuality.'

There was another door at the top of the stairs which opened onto a hall with high ceilings and plaster mouldings. The floorboards creaked as they moved around.

The kitchen had a gas stove with four rings and an oven. It was well used but looked as if it had had a professional clean; no fatty residues in the oven, and the burners looked as if they'd work.

'Unfortunately, you can't test the facilities. All power is off because it's not occupied. We don't want squatters or any other freeloaders. I can assure you, though, that everything works.' Meredith and Calvin nodded approvingly.

The bathroom was similarly functional: a bright pink suite of shower over bath, toilet, and wash-hand basin.

The four bedrooms were all decent-sized. They'd just about accommodate a double bed. The sitting room had plenty of dralon and thin, shabby curtains. All in shades of beige.

Meredith asked, 'Who's downstairs?'

Poole said, 'Group of students. They've all rented separately, so I don't think they're a group. I've had no trouble with them—no late-night parties, no calls from the police. You have no idea how valuable that is to a landlord.'

Meredith said, 'This looks fine. We've got a couple of others to look at. We'll let you know by the end of today.'

At 4 p.m., after visiting a couple of other places, Meredith reported back to Else. She put on her Dr Martens and walked around the local streets.

'Yes, it looks good. Lots of people who are likely to be unobservant and probably unwilling to remember too much should the cops come calling. Sort it out. I'm going back to the safety of south London.'

Meredith phoned Poole to take the flat and agreed to meet again the following day to sign papers, hand over a deposit, and give the first month's rent.

Calvin said, 'I don't fancy sleeping on those mattresses... Who knows what might be living in them.'

Meredith replied, 'Yes, let's go buy some decent mattresses. I don't think Else will worry about it.'

The next day, Meredith and Calvin were sitting in their new flat, looking out of the massive bay windows.

Meredith went downstairs and used the payphone in the entrance hall to phone Else.

'Get down to that pub. If there's anyone dealing, deal with them. Daryl and me want it to be real clear that there's a new team in town.'

***

Ember sat in his flat above the off-licence. It looked out over the front of the shop into the street. He accessed it using the stairs from inside the shop. It adjoined old Eric's former abode.

He was looking at the pile of money. He'd seen lots of money before, but it felt different now that he was sitting at home and could just lean forward and touch it. It would have looked naff to have done so with Loxton and Tacette there. He had to play it cool, just put the money away and walk off nonchalantly.

But now, the notes seemed to grow in front of his eyes, and he couldn't stop himself from picking them up, giving them a bit of a riffle, and then putting them down, only to repeat the exercise a few moments later. He knew, of course, that this was exactly why Loxton and Tacette had brought along folding money. Promises, guarantees, assurances – none carried the same clout as having the notes there in front of him.

In some ways, the presence of the notes highlighted one of the practicalities. If he wanted to launder the cash through the off-licence, he could possibly hide fifty quid a day, but even that amount could draw attention on an average daily take of a hundred quid. If he lowered the laundering to twenty quid a day, it would take over three years to get rid of it and, of course, there'd be more coming in.

Loxton and Tacette were right. If he was going to be part of their alliance, he'd have to have a new business where he could establish higher trading figures from the start.

But did he want to be mixed up with these low-lifes? The risks worried him. Drug dealing was often life-ending for users and dealers alike. That's why he'd got out of it as soon as he could. But the risks to life were as nothing when compared to the malign spirit of Iles and his mate Harpur. They seemed to have the ability to prod the sensitive parts, and he didn't want any more prodding from their direction.

On the other hand, it was money for old rope. They'd give him the cash. He'd put it through a till and then find ways to channel eighty-five per cent back to them. This could be reliable, copious funding. He'd not have to worry about trade or going bust.

On balance, with the twenty grand continuing to grow in his eyes, he felt that he should accept the offer. He wondered whether he could negotiate a better percentage. Clearly, they wanted him, so maybe.

***

Tacette, Loxton, and Ember sat at a table in The Montague Club. It was a fine building just off the docks. When the docks were the lifeblood of trade in the area, the Monty had been the haunt of boat owners in the lounge area and ship hands in the public bar. It had panelled walls and high ceilings – remnants of a bygone Victorian style.

In its time, it had been a monument to the success of the port and its place as the supplier of wealth to the city and the towns and villages beyond.

But those times were long gone. The port still operated for smaller freighters and some dredgers. The cranes sat on their tracks but rarely moved. The rail tracks that were set in concrete and criss-crossed the roads were no longer inconvenienced by trains.

The huge warehouses were slowly being taken down; there was no redevelopment, but the dangers posed by these massive, unmaintained buildings meant that they had to be destroyed. There were endless expanses of flat concrete where warehouses and factories had been but were now voids, speaking of the passing of an era and the awaited arrival of a new one.

The Monty was visited by locals after slightly cheaper booze, interspersed with working girls taking it easy between shifts and small-time dealers looking for a less public place for their trade. The erosion of the place appalled Ember; it spoke so clearly of decay and hopelessness.

Loxton and Tacette saw it as a convenient and moderately private place where they could speak freely without the fear of being overheard.

Tacette said, 'So, what do you think about our proposal?'

Ember, reminding himself of the piles of notes, said, 'I think it could work. But even cleaning up that money will take ages in my offie. We need to think about a new business venture, something that is cash-based. I don't want cheques; too traceable and auditable. Tax men love that sort of thing, and that could pique the interest of the local constables. And I am taking some considerable risks... Remember Al Capone? Done for tax fraud, not for anything criminal.'

Tacette interrupted, 'Ralphy, old mate, don't try to up your share. You's doing very well out of it as it is… Lots of cash for doing fuck all.'

Loxton looked like he had an idea. 'What about a pub or a club? Nobody uses cheques there. All good, clean cash.'

Ember went to the bar and ordered three Armagnacs. The barman was in his fifties or sixties, with grey swept-back hair. He was carrying considerable weight, gathered into a barrel-shaped paunch that balanced on thin legs, making him look like a very large, well-nourished robin.

'Can't remember the last time anyone ordered one of those, let alone three. I'll need me steps to get to the back of the shelf to get the bottle out. But I 'spect it matures with age; if it do, it'll be real splendid!'

Ember sat with Tacette and Loxton, sipping his brandy. The other two babbled on about arrangements and details. He was in another place, dreaming of a time when he was a truly respected member of local society—a voice, an opinion sought by important decision-makers.

'So, what do you think of that?'

But Ember hadn't heard a word of Loxton's conversation.

Ember spoke quietly and slowly, allowing his ideas to form. 'What about this place? It has a certain grandeur. Definitely seen better days; the décor hasn't had attention in decades, and I reckon the fabric of the building will need some long-term and expensive attention. The clientele could do with cleaning up, too, but all in good time.'

Tacette said, 'Yes. I like the idea of long-term, expensive repairs. That could hide a multitude of sins.'

Ember went back to the bar.

'Who owns this place?'

The barman took a deep breath and said, 'I do. Retired from the cops. Took my pension money and sunk it in here. Must have been fucking mad. When I bought it, there was lots of talk of clearing the slums and factories and building a marina. I'd have been quids in. But Thatcher put an end to all that. There's no money for nothing round here, and it's all decaying around my ears. I'm just about surviving, but only because I let the local entrepreneurs conduct business here.'

Ember said, 'Would you sell?'

The barman replied, 'In a shot. But who'd buy it, and for how much? I've got a lot of money sunk in it.'

Ember left and drove back to his shop. He opened up for the afternoon business. After he closed, he went back to the Monty. There were more people in there, but the same type of clientele.

As he walked in, one of the working girls caught his eye and allowed her gaze to wander all over his body. He stood by the bar, giving her his profile; the way he felt he most resembled Charlton Heston.

She sidled over and said, 'Fancy buying me a drink?'

Ember bought himself a half of lager and a gin and tonic for the girl.

They sat at a table.

'So, who are you, gorgeous?'

Ember replied, 'Ralph. I just dropped in to speak to the barman. What's your name?'

'I'm Desiré. I come here quite a lot. Haven't seen you before. I do good rates for someone good-looking, someone with a bit of class.'

Ember replied, 'That's good to hear. Wouldn't want you charging the same rate for fat, ugly people.'

They laughed at the ridiculousness of the idea.

They finished their drinks, and Ember went back to the bar. The barman was looking lonely as he turned the pages of *The Post*.

'What sort of money would you want for the place? I've had a bit of good fortune and might be interested, if the price is right.'

'I would only want enough to get out and be able to live out my retirement in some luxury—a place to live, the occasional holiday, a visit to the pub a couple of evenings a week.'

Ember said, 'Would thirty-five grand do it? This place needs a lot of work, not just on jollying up inside, but shoring up some big and expensive repairs outside.'

The barman said, 'Chuck in another two and a half and you've got a deal.'

Ember exclaimed, 'Fantastic! I can see a bright future for both of us.'

Chapter 16

Harpur was battling against the wind again as the channel siphoned air off the ocean and compressed it into a freezing jet directed straight at him. He could see why Lamb always liked meeting here; it was unobserved, especially at this time of year. It could be bright, but it was always breezy.

Lamb appeared wearing more army-surplus gear. This time, he had a short leather jacket, called a bumfreezer. He had well-pressed khaki-green trousers tucked into his wellies.

'Thanks for meeting so quickly. I thought you might like to know about some business developments.'

'I'm always interested in how our entrepreneurs are exploiting business opportunities,' Harpur replied.

'I've heard that some local entrepreneurs are worried,' Lamb said. 'They are thinking my enemy's enemy is my friend. So they are joining forces, so to speak. Interestingly, they've been seen talking to Mister Ralph W. Ember pillar of society and local businessman.'

Harpur felt obliged to wheedle for more information—who said it and where they were seen—but Lamb cut the discussion short. 'I like to look out to sea and imagine the Nazis trying to make a landing whilst our brave boys repelled them from these concrete coffins. Makes you proud, doesn't it?'

'Yes. Funny how we have to look back to be proud,' Harpur said.

***

At The Monty, Ember had called Jack Veness over to the table with Loxton and Tacette. Ember described his plans.

'My friends here have lots of experience in business, and I'm keen on their advice in relation to The Monty. I think we provisionally agreed on thirty-seven and a half?' he asked, concerned that he had allowed his excitement to overtake his good sense and that Tacette and Loxton might not see the business opportunity he did.

'This is an area ripe for development,' Tacette said. 'It has been neglected and left to fall into the hands of hookers and dealers. Such an august presence as Ralphy here would change perceptions and be a draw for investors. Which is not to say that your efforts to raise the class of the area have been totally in vain, Jack.' Tacette looked around vainly for evidence of some form of success in raising the class.

'I can see real potential here,' Loxton joined in. 'Ralph, this will, of course, be your venture, but you can rely on our support.'

Ember left The Monty in high spirits. He popped down to the Esplanade to see if he could find Desiré again; he felt he needed someone to share the success with. He found her in an alleyway, her thin, straggly coat pulled up tight around her, her bare legs pink in the cold, poking out below. She got into his car and they went back to his flat. He was not worried about her knowing his address; this was to become part of his past. The moments with tarts in tawdry flats above barely profitable off-licences were about to be in the past. He was to be a gentleman of the area, a respected person who was the impresario who brought good things to the area through his stewardship of The Monty. Such a substantial institution, as a building and as a members' club, did not lend itself to ownership.

No, Ralph W. Ember would merely oversee it, develop it, nurture it and then pass it on to the next person to take up the mantle. He saw this as a noble mission.

The following morning, Ember knocked on the window of a shop front on the opposite side of the road from his off-licence. The window hadn't been cleaned in a long time, and it was difficult to see through. Posters inside described the various services offered – housing advice, immigration appeals, crime, and accident compensation. Above was a hand-painted sign: Latimer and Associates, Legal Services.

Carl Latimer was known to almost everyone as "Curvy Carl" because he wasn't felt to be completely bent. He made most of his living by representing the local hookers and dealers, claiming legal aid. He had never really had any associates, and he definitely didn't now. Those who had worked with him had found the endless series of soliciting, possession and dealing work too dull and too poorly paid. Curvy Carl couldn't remember the last time he'd had an uninterrupted night—his regulars were often getting nicked and demanding their legal advice, whatever time of day or night, generally night. The legal advice was always the same: 'Say nothing.'

Sometimes he went to the station to give the same advice. Every now and then, a new client would pop up but the advice was generally the same. He spent a significant part of the daylight at court delivering heartfelt pleas for clemency. It usually ended up with a fine, which meant the client would have to go back to the trade they plied to pay off the fine, and round it would all go. But it paid the bills, just about.

He opened the door to Ember. He noticed straight away that this was not his usual type of client.

'How can I help you?' Curvy asked.

Ember sat in an office chair in front of Curvy's desk. There were lots of lockable filing cabinets sitting on well-worn lino tiles. On the walls were various certificates in frames—no longer straight and breaking up the tired-looking magnolia paint. Ember imagined that the office had opened about a decade before with brand-new paint, certificates, level and proud, with the owner excited about the good he was going to do in this under-privileged area. Then reality had snuck in. It had leeched colour and pride; it had stolen ambition and idealism. You can only help those who can help themselves and want to do it.

Curvy was in the small kitchen at the back of the office. He came back with two mugs of tea. He was wearing a dark grey suit that might once have been black. An off-white shirt provided the backdrop for a blue polyester tie. The soles of his black shoes were worn on the outside, the result of his pronated walking style. The leather showed areas of light grey, indicating the places most in need of polish.

'Sorry about the milk, I'm not here all that often, so only keep sterilised milk here. What can I do for you?' he said.

Ember sipped the foul tea. 'Wow, what have you done to deserve tea like this?' They laughed.

'No, I shouldn't be ungrateful. Thanks for the tea. I have a slightly delicate matter that I wish to discuss.'

Ember described his plans to buy The Monty.

'That all seems perfectly straightforward,' Curvy said. 'I think you might need someone with more experience in business-property transactions. It's not exactly my forte, but if you are set on me dealing with it, I can promise you lots of endeavour and willingness to work.'

'Yes, I think you are someone I'd like to work with on this. I see myself as a bastion of the local community, someone who could use his influence, however small, to encourage businesses around here to flourish and support general improvements. Part of that has to be a commitment to local businesses in the form of trade. To put it more succinctly, I think I should use someone local for this work.'

'Very noble,' Curvy replied, waiting for the real reason to reveal itself.

'There is, of course, a slight complication. A significant amount of the money will come in cash. As you can imagine, with my successful off-licence business across the road, I receive lots of cash and I've been less than fastidious in getting it paid into the bank. All above board, of course, but the sudden purchase of a large building using folding material could draw attention.'

'I see the problem. How much cash?' Curvy asked.

Ember stood up and walked around the office. 'Perhaps we shouldn't talk figures until we are clearer about the basis on which we will transact business. The total cost is thirty-seven and a half. Lots of it will come from banked holdings, but some will be of the nature I described.'

'I receive cash payments from my more prosperous clients and I lodge it in the client account,' Curvy said. 'I think it's fair to say that I haven't had too many prosperous clients of late, but I think there could be a few about to seek my advice, if you catch my drift. You know, looking at opportunities around the docks?'

'Excellent. Lovely to hear of the interest of people from outside the area in business opportunities here. I hope that they will firm up their interests very soon and that your excellent advice will be needed similarly, very soon,' Ember said.

'I expect the first might be dropping in tomorrow, if that helps?' Curvy replied.

The following day, Ralph visited Curvy and handed over some of the cash from Tacette and Loxton.

'I can't tell you how disappointed me and my associates would be if any of this money went missing.'

'I can assure you of the security of all my dealings and will only deduct the agreed fee,' Curvy replied.

Chapter 17

'The Home Sec wants a full inquiry. He's after transparency and accountability. Jeavons was lapping it all up, suggesting that he could have a significant role in the democratic side of things. It was vomit-inducing stuff—as if his 1,500 votes at the last council elections gives him any democratic credibility at all. And I expect you can imagine who has been suggested as the force to carry out the inquiry, the Mason-hating shower from up the road. He said he thought they'd have a head start, having already been investigating Inspector Fletcher. Now they have the complete remit to look for all sorts of spooks, ghouls and other apparitions that might be evidence of Masonic influence in the decision-making.'

The ACC shifted in his seat. 'I've been through my notes and I feel confident that I have the evidence to justify every decision.'

Iles raised his eyebrows. 'Not sure that this will be about evidence and justification.'

***

Tacette, Loxton and Ember were at a table at The Monty.

'I've paid over a deposit, and Curvy is on the case, sorting out the freehold and other details. This should all happen pretty quickly. We've worked out how to disguise the origins.'

Ember leaned back and looked around the bar, making plans in his head.

'Me and Leo have a bit of a problem that we hopes you can help us with,' Loxton said.

Ember's moment of basking came to an abrupt end.

'You've probably 'eard of the problems that Copsey and the old git suffered? Our info is that this is some out-of-towners trying to muscle in on our trade. We knows that you'd be real upset about violence and conflict being brought to our lovely town, not to mention the potential impact on our income!'

'We need to send a very clear message back to them. A sort of "fuck off" RSVP. But it needs to be equally loud as theirs was to us. We knows you got some experience of solving these sorts of problems. We thought about using our own people, but this is above their experience. When we was discussing it, we was talking about anyone we know who've got the skills and experience. There's no one at your level, Ralphy, and, as an encouragement to ensure the safety of our dealing arrangement, we wondered if you would show your commitment by taking on a little message-sending work,' Tacette said.

'I'm trying to stay out of that sort of thing now—I'm a pillar of society, a local businessman, letters in the paper,' Ember protested.

'But a local businessman helping to launder drugs money, a pillar of society with some very questionable previous dealings,' Loxton pointed out. 'And, anyway, Ralphy, you can't have thought we was giving you the money just for buying The Monty? Not even you is that daft.'

Ember touched his scar. He could feel the symptoms of panic rising within him. He breathed in deeply and exhaled slowly and felt the panic subside. He was pleased with himself—he had managed to hide the panic from Loxton and Tacette, and he was able to continue the conversation in a calm way.

'What is it you want me to do?' he asked.

'Our information is that a London firm wants to move in,' Tacette said. 'They've got a couple of their boys lodging down in the student area. I think one of them needs to come to an unfortunate end, and the other needs to find him. That way, we gets rid of one of them and makes the other shit scared that it could happen to him.'

***

Harpur was in his office, going through the endless pile of crime reports, when Iles walked in.

'We need to come up with something for the chief on the two investigations. We've got some leads. I wonder if we should take things into the hornets' nest, if you'll pardon the damage to a perfectly good metaphor. I think something a little off the books—I don't think we want to be telling the Met or the chief anything about it.'

Harpur booked out a brown Morris Marina. Iles got in wearing jeans and a polo shirt. Harpur was wearing his usual style of business suit.

'I'm hoping to project informality and approachability by the casual attire. You do that naturally, whatever you wear,' Iles said.

'We need to leave them with the understanding that the doors of our town are not open to any Tom, Dick or Harriet to come along and ply their despicable trade. And talking of despicable trade, have you had the chance to discuss Garland's behaviour?' Iles continued.

Harpur concentrated on driving but could feel the temperature rising as Iles' voice rose in volume.

'I don't think that Garland or you understand how much I love Sarah. In a way, her waywardness makes me love her more. But that doesn't mean that a colleague can take advantage of her waywardness. I hope you have conveyed that to him.'

His words became louder and more staccato with less melting of one into another. Harpur thought it a good moment to change the subject.

'I hear that Tacette and Loxton have joined forces and have included Ember.'

'Where have you heard this? More off-record informery?'

'Yes, I've heard it somewhere. Could be useful if they find a way to keep the London crowd out. Maybe it's some conflict we could resolve between us?'

'I can't see that lot being able to compete with a well-organised metropolitan outfit, even with the noble Ralph Ember. They may well need the beneficent intervention of the local constabulary,' Iles replied.

They pulled up outside Else Philipson's house on the outskirts of South London.

Harpur rang the doorbell. Else opened it, and Iles pushed past.

'A visit from your not-so-local cops. We want to have a chat, off the record,' Iles said.

'Who the fuck are you?' Else asked.

Meredith was in her front room. Iles sat, uninvited, on her settee. Harpur joined him.

'We're the old bill—I think that's the charming term for police you use down here. We're investigating the deaths of chaps called Drummond and Foreshaw,' Harpur said.

'We don't know nothing about it,' Meredith said. Else shot him a look. He sat back in his chair.

'As my colleague said, we know nothing of these matters,' Else added.

'I expected that to be the case,' Iles continued.

'What would be the case?' Else asked.

'That you would say that you know nothing of these matters. Let me be very clear. We are onto you. We will use all resources at our disposal to get to you. Our colleagues at the Met will be similarly committed. We will all, of course, operate within the law where possible,' Iles said.

'Where possible?' Else repeated.

'Definitely within the law, where possible. I think you'd expect nothing less. If you look at my colleague, you'll see that he has a history of operating within the law where possible. If you look at me, you'll think that it's been possible for me to operate within the law more often. Looks can be deceiving,' Iles replied.

'We'd be very concerned if there were any suggestion of external factors affecting local businesses in our area,' Harpur added.

'You are just trying to shore up the trade for your own people—you getting a nice cut, are you? Well, let me be clear. We, by which I mean my associate and I, have no connection to any illegal activity.

But, if we did, this half-arsed warning from some cops of a rural force would not be something to make us remotely worried,' Else said.

'That's a shame. It's never good to make enemies of the cops, wherever they come from,' Iles said.

On the way back, Harpur said, 'The conflict continues.'

'They don't know what they're dealing with. I don't think they've dealt with a police force so committed to protecting its communities. The chief has really rubbed off on me,' Iles smiled.

Chapter 18

Ember's phone rang in his flat.

'Ralphy, I hope all is well with you,' Loxton said. 'I have some interesting information for you to help you with our business arrangement. Perhaps we could have a brief meeting at our usual place?'

At The Monty, Ember sat at the bar. He'd put on some decent trousers and a proper button-up shirt. He wanted to start to raise the standards of the clientele and felt that he should demonstrate the dress code that would apply soon, after he had formally taken over control. He was sipping a half of Hofmeister lager. It was bracingly cold, but not cold enough to disguise the absence of flavour and body. When he took over, Ralph would bring in proper, premium lager—maybe some Stella Artois. It was advertised as being 'reassuringly expensive.' Just the sort of thing the new Monty needed.

He wanted to be fully with it for the meeting with Loxton. Loxton appeared dressed in jeans and a T-shirt. Ember felt this was disappointing, that Loxton should at least try to reflect the improved nature of the club.

Ember got him a Coke, and they went to a table.

'Benny, I've been thinking about this job. I'm not sure it fits with my stature.'

'Ralphy, we've had the discussion and explained it all to you. You can't take the dosh and not do the work—we're also most concerned to get you close and personal to our business, just in case you ever have to consider your loyalties, you know, if our esteemed friend Mr Iles should pop around, sticking his fucking nose in where it don't belong.'

'OK. What can you tell me?'

'We heard that a couple of out-of-town people have taken a house in the student area. I'll give you the number of the car, so you just got to drive around, find it and wait for them to appear.'

'Jesus, that could take weeks. What if they're not there? What if they've changed the car? I've got a business to run.'

'I expect you'll find a way,' Loxton replied. 'You got twenty grand to help you along, haven't you?'

***

Ember began searching the student area, going up and down, looking for a nondescript Escort among the lines of other nondescript cars. He had a couple of hours before he opened the off-licence. The car wouldn't be parked all the time, so even if he didn't find it in the streets he searched, that didn't mean it wouldn't be parked there later. This meant the task of finding it was going to be long and repetitive. He didn't want to get any help either. The fewer people who knew about the job, the better, not to mention not having to spend some of the money from Tacette and Loxton.

It worried him that Tacette and Loxton would view failure on his part as evidence of him panicking. He wasn't taken in by the patronising bollocks about him being professional and experienced. They were justifying getting him involved in something very serious so that they could rely on his continuing support. On the other hand,

143

failure to do the job could lead to him being demoted from the respected position he had earned and being more patronised and bullied, probably leading to a smaller share of profits.

He found himself in a very uncomfortable position, having to do a job that he really didn't have the stomach for, but not being able to do it half-arsed because of the impact on his future.

For several days, he drove up and down the same streets. He'd broken the area into sections so that he wouldn't be on the same streets too often. He hoped this would make sure he wasn't spotted. He had a white Morris 1800, so not something that should attract attention.

***

It was 7.30 on Saturday morning. Harpur's phone rang. Meghan was in bed next to him.

'Often get calls at this time?'

'No, I'll need to get it. Could be important.'

Harpur picked up the phone and heard Lamb's voice say, 'Ember is on manoeuvres.' The line went dead.

Harpur dropped by Iles's house. It was a double-fronted Victorian with large sash windows. Iles opened the door in a long satin dressing gown.

'How lovely to see you on this fine morning. Do come in. Sarah is upstairs, and I'm sure she'll join us soon.'

'I've heard that Ember is up to something.'

'I shan't bother trying to explore where this information comes from,' Iles said.

Sarah joined them in the front room, hugging a mug of coffee. She was wearing a long negligee that gathered around her hips and breasts. Harpur carefully avoided gazing for too long. He wondered if he'd detected her eyes resting on him a moment too long. Or was it just wishful thinking?

'Lovely to see you. Just talking a bit of business with Des.'

'And he'll be leaving very soon,' Iles said.

Chapter 19

Iles was wearing all black as he drove around the student quarter. He knew it was a long shot, but if Ember was out and about in the area, he felt duty-bound to see if he could find him. It was one of those challenges that reminded him of his early career, trying to catch burglars—trying to get inside their heads to understand how they might operate and what they would do to make sure they weren't caught.

As he drove down St Edwards Terrace, he caught a glimpse of the Charlton Heston profile. Ember was standing in an alleyway, a few feet back from the road, so that any light emitted from the street lights didn't reach him. Iles drove on and parked several streets away and retraced his route back, using doorways and cars as cover.

He managed to find a way into the same alley as Ember, but further away from the road. Iles could see that Ember was doing his own surveillance operation.

Ember was relieved. He'd been getting despondent, worrying about how he was going to find the car and what Tacette and Loxton would make of any failure on his part. They had said that they viewed him as an experienced professional, and he was happy for them to use that description. It was better than 'Panicking Ralph.' But he could do without them calling him 'Ralphy'—that made him sound juvenile and insubstantial. When he'd done this job, he'd put them straight.

It was getting late and cold. But having found the car, he couldn't take the risk of leaving it. He paced back and forth across the alleyway, rubbing his hands and stamping his feet. He wished he'd dressed better for a night in the cold.

Further up the alley, Iles kept in the shadows. He'd foreseen the likelihood of a long night out in the open and wore enough layers to keep warm. He also had a foil package of sandwiches.

As Ember paced, a door in one of the houses opposite opened, and a man walked across the road to the car. He opened the boot, took out a bag and went back into number five. Ember kept watching and saw the curtains on the first floor close.

Following Dawn's surveillance, Ember surmised that there would probably be two people present, and he needed to either split them up or wait for them to split up, allowing him to target one on his own. He checked that he had his knife in one pocket and a gun in the other. Even though it was a large house and the other occupants would probably be students, so untroubled by pops and bangs, he preferred to avoid the risk of cops getting called. He planned to do the job with his knife, but recognised that, unless he was able to maintain the advantage of surprise, he would have to use his gun. He had a silencer, but he couldn't put that on with the gun being kept inside his jacket because it was too long, and the gun butt would create a very obvious bulge that could draw attention.

He settled down for a long night of observation. He'd heard the police refer to this as 'lifestyle'—understanding how a target for surveillance lived, making it easier to pick them up when an operation started. Ember didn't need to know about lifestyle for surveillance. He needed to know when he could strike one of them when alone.

He was satisfied with himself because he didn't feel panic rising in him. He congratulated himself on how he'd become more balanced and calm under this sort of pressure. This was exactly why Tacette and Loxton saw him as the experienced professional, the only person who could take on this task. He chose to ignore Loxton's uncharitable suggestion that they were making sure he wouldn't grass on them because he was too caught up in their criminality.

At around 5 a.m., after a cold night watching unmoving curtains and dark windows at number five, the front door opened. The man who had visited the car the night before appeared in lurid running gear— day-glo yellow vest and expensive-looking trainers. He looked at his watch and trotted off.

Ember considered options. He could wait to see how long the runner was away, so the next time he'd know how long he'd got. But that would mean another extended period of surveillance with all the risks that posed. He also thought that waiting would make the task itself more and more significant in his mind, increasing the probability of incapacitating terror when the moment came. Moving now meant he'd not know how long he'd got, but he wasn't planning to hang around, and, with a bit of luck, the other person would be present and still asleep in bed.

He pulled up his hood over his woolly hat and crossed the road. As he suspected, the front door looked substantial but was secured with a feeble Yale lock. He slid a piece of washing-up bottle between the frame and the door, releasing the lock. Inside, he found himself in a hall with another, less substantial-looking door to his right. He did the same trick as he'd done on the front door and moved on to the stairway. He shut the door behind him. The staircase was narrow and enclosed. There was a weak light, and he climbed the stairs slowly, taking one step at a time and trying to make as little noise as possible. The carpet was thin, but it cushioned his feet on each stair. He was wearing soft-soled trainers—he'd anticipated the need for quiet operation. He'd calculated that if he needed heavy boots, it had probably gone wrong.

At the top of the stairs, he came to another door. This door had no lock, so he pulled the handle down and pushed it open. He stood still for a couple of minutes, looking and listening for signs of life. It was still dark, but Ember's eyes had adjusted. He could see a landing with doors off it, all closed. He leaned through the door to get a good look at all the doors. He knew the room to the left would be the front room, so the last one he'd look at. He could also work out that the room next to it would have to be a kitchen or bathroom, because of the proximity of the doors on either side. This still left five other doors. He stepped onto the landing and made his way towards the door at the furthest right, reasoning that sleeping quarters would be furthest from the living room. He was going to have to make a swift but noiseless entry to each room. He left the landing door open in case he needed to make a rapid exit. He held his knife in front of him, the blade pointing forward between thumb and forefinger.

His scar was throbbing again, as if it had opened up. He could feel the sweat beginning to roll down his back. He knew he had to move quickly to prevent a complete breakdown.

As he entered the landing, he heard a cry from behind him, and Meredith appeared from a small void behind the staircase. The cry was intended to disorientate and cause panic and fear. Meredith held a knife above his head in his right hand. He ran at Ralph, bringing the knife down towards his back. The cry gave Ralph a moment to turn around. He saw Meredith running at him, the muscles in his face drawn tight and his right arm held high, ready to strike. As the knife came down with speed and force, Ralph stepped to the side and received a glancing blow that cut through his coat and nicked his right upper arm. The momentum carried Meredith past Ember along the landing. He turned to have another go and ran back towards Ember. Ember put up his left hand and caught Meredith's wrist, deflecting the knife away from him. Meredith's momentum carried him into Ember, and they collided with some force.

The expression on Meredith's face changed, and he stepped back. Ember could see the handle of his knife protruding from Meredith's stomach. Ember was bemused and relieved at the speed at which the knife had incapacitated Meredith.

Meredith fell to his knees and then twisted to the side to avoid falling forward onto the knife. He lay on his side. His breathing became laboured and he made a gurgling sound. Ember wondered whether blood would come from his mouth—he had always wondered why an abdominal injury led to blood coming from the mouth. Maybe it was just done for dramatic effect in films. No blood came from Meredith.

Ember felt he had to finish the job straight away. He couldn't take the risk that Meredith would survive. He didn't want to take the knife out and plunge it into him again—that was all too close and personal, not to mention messy.

He drew his gun and screwed on the silencer. He thought about the potential for a bullet passing straight through Meredith's head and hitting someone in the rooms below. There was no need to endanger an innocent bystander. The cops and juries could look very dimly on such things. He went into the kitchen to get a frying pan—he'd put that under Meredith's head and then shoot straight down. That way, there'd be no risk of "over-penetration." He liked that euphemism—it sounded sophisticated, yet the event itself that could cause "over-penetration" was so brutal and unsophisticated.

In the kitchen, he found the cupboard of saucepans and took out a frying pan. The adrenaline of the fight was wearing off, and he could feel the advancing panic. His hands were shaking, and his breathing had become shallow and fast. He could feel his heart leaping up and down in his chest. He was feeling sick and felt that his legs could no longer hold him up. He was sure the scar had opened up, and he expected to feel blood dripping down his face.

He took a chair from the kitchen and went on to the landing. He sat on the chair with the frying pan in one hand and the gun in the other.

He closed his eyes, unable to hold them open because of the stress. He sat there shivering and tense, stroking his scar, making sure it wasn't bleeding.

He felt the frying pan move, but he knew no one could be there—he'd have heard the door opening. It was just his brain playing tricks. But he knew he couldn't stay any longer. He opened his eyes. Meredith was on his back. The frying pan was under his head, and there was a neat hole in his forehead. His gun was in Ember's hand and smelled of burning.

He concluded that, experienced as he was in these types of stressful situations, he had gone into automatic mode and completed the task, almost without knowing it.

He left, shutting all doors.

Chapter 20

The chief was looking even more tired and drawn. He'd called a crisis meeting. Harpur, Iles and the ACC were there, as were the head of crime and the head of communications. The chief's secretary sat at the end of the table making notes.

'I can't understand how this keeps happening. Another murder—and please don't tell me it might not be a murder. I might not have been a detective for very long, but even I know that a stab wound to the stomach and a bullet hole in the forehead rule out suicide. The Post, Home Secretary and Jeavons are all going to have a field day with this.'

The head of crime, Detective Chief Superintendent Lyle, stood to give his update. He was a stout man with a face that spoke of a thousand pints and a thousand late nights. He was jowly with a rubescent complexion. His suit was crumpled and well-worn, reflecting the wearer with incredible accuracy.

'The body was found by Mr Michael Poole. He owns the premises and had rented it out to two people. They had paid in cash. The names they gave have turned out to be false, and all the other details lead nowhere. The deceased had a deep knife wound to the stomach. He had continued to bleed for some time after being stabbed, meaning that the shot to the forehead was what actually killed him. We think he'd been dead for a couple of days when he was found. There are no useful marks anywhere in the flat—it has been very efficiently cleaned. We've taken the victim's prints and he has been identified as a bloke called Meredith. All his offending was in London. We've spoken to the Met and they have him linked to an organised crime group called the Philipsons. So this looks like some sort of gang fight.'

'We need to get something out that suggests we have this all under control, that we know what's going on, that an arrest or arrests are imminent and that there is no risk to the public,' the chief said.

'That's quite a tall order. I'll work with the ACC and Des to draft something up,' the head of comms said.

***

Ember sat with Tacette and Loxton at their usual table at The Monty.

'Very impressive piece of work, Ralphy, very impressive. Exactly what we needed—clear message, delivered first hand to one of their own.'

Ember sat back in his chair and sipped on the Armagnac that Tacette had bought.

'You said it, you needed someone professional and experienced. I think we can stop the "Ralphy" bit now, please—it's just Ralph. I'll get on with setting up The Monty.'

Iles and Harpur walked in.

'What a fine gathering, wouldn't you say, Col?' They drew up chairs and joined the three at the table. 'Brandy at eleven in the morning? Are you celebrating?'

'Well, yes,' Ember replied. 'I've decided to take over The Monty here. As you know, I have ambitions for this area. I want to create a place where upstanding members of the community can come to

153

discuss business or relax from the vicissitudes of a hard day's work. A place for like-minded people to enjoy a relaxed environment, away from the hurly-burly of a pub or nightclub.'

'How very exciting. Colin and I are always supportive of local improvements, and we'll be pleased to drop in, from time to time, to show our support.'

Ember forced a smile. 'Lovely, I'll look forward to it.'

'While we're here, I wonder whether you might be able to throw any light on an investigation we're conducting—when I say "we," I mean "we the police," not "we, Colin and me." Have you heard of a murder in the student quarter?'

Tacette felt it best if he handled this conversation. 'I'd heard about it—read it in the paper. We haven't discussed it because, of course, we have no knowledge about it. Do you notice the way in which denials always sound so weak? But the truth of the matter is that this tragic event is of no interest, concern or import to us, so we haven't had need to discuss it.'

'That's interesting. There is a witness who says that they saw a male hanging around an alleyway.'

Ember made sure his face didn't change expression, and he maintained his gaze across the bar. Iles looked at him.

'I wonder if any of you are in the habit of hanging around in alleyways in the student quarter or know anyone who might be?'

'I can't speak for my friends, but I'd feel confident in saying it is unlikely. Was this witness able to identify this person?'

'We'll run them through the mugshots,' Harpur said, looking directly at Ember, 'but it was dark and the witness was obviously not contemplating that the person might be involved in murder, so wasn't looking to be able to identify him later. I don't expect that he'll make an identification.'

'That's unfortunate—whatever the person's history, they don't deserve to be murdered.'

'That's a very uplifting observation. I think I can say that Colin and I would agree with you almost wholeheartedly.'

Harpur and Iles left.

In the car, Harpur said, 'I was talking to the lead investigator. That witness saw two people. One had the profile of Charlton Heston—remind you of anyone?'

'Yes, that could be Ember, but I don't think he'll get picked out.'

'And there was a second person, taller. This person was much better at staying in the shadows, so no chance of an identification.' Harpur kept his eyes on the road. 'I wonder who that might be?'

'Yes, I wonder,' Iles replied. 'Of course, neither might have been involved. I don't think that hanging around in alleyways is an offence. I think we should make a repeat visit to Else Philipson. I'd like to gauge how she sees the future.'

They drove to London. It was a bright and cold day with frost on the pavements. Iles was in well-cut jeans again, Harpur adequately contained by his suit. They parked in a residential street in Streatham and walked the ten minutes to Else's house. She answered the door wearing jeans and a blue striped blouse. She had well-applied makeup.

'How lovely to see you again,' Iles said as he walked in uninvited.

'What are you doing here? I thought I made it clear at your last visit that we don't have anything to discuss.'

'But that's where you're wrong.' Iles spoke as if about to announce a large lottery win. 'We have so much to discuss. Colin and I are doing a bit of background work for a murder investigation.'

'Would this murder investigation involve someone called Meredith?'

'How very perspicacious. Exactly right. I suspect that you might be about to tell us that you've spoken to our esteemed colleagues from the Met and told them that you don't know anything of Meredith's circumstances and that his death came as a surprise to you. Of course, we know a bit differently, don't we?' Iles winked conspiratorially, as if sharing a secret.

'I seem to remember he was here when we visited last time, so someone quite well known to you,' Harpur added. 'We're wondering if there's anything you can tell us about his living arrangements. Anything that might explain why he got a knife in his stomach and a bullet in his head. It's not the type of thing that usually befalls the average member of the public. So we're wondering if you can help us identify why he might not have been an average member of the public.'

'Of course, I knew him,' Else replied. 'He was a friend. I don't know anything about his, how should I put it, circumstances. I'd like to be able to help—I'd want to help catch the person or people responsible for this savagery.'

'That's interesting—you mention the possibility of "people,"' Iles said. 'What makes you think that more than one person might be involved?'

'It's interesting that you have focused on the possibility of more than one person rather than a single person being responsible. Do you know more than you're letting on? The Met detective who spoke to me said that two people were seen near the scene. One seemed nervous and, as it turned out, could have been watching Mr Meredith's place. The second person was much taller and seemed considerably less agitated.' She looked over at Iles and, involuntarily, her eyebrows lifted.

Harpur noticed the change in expression. 'Yes, we are obviously aware of that information. We fear that the witness will be unlikely to identify those people and, of course, they may be unconnected. We have put out witness appeals on posters as well as on our local TV and radio. No one has come forward as yet, but we remain hopeful. If those two people came forward, we could eliminate them.'

'These are routine types of steps that you would expect any competent police force to take,' Iles added. 'We're here because we want to go beyond the routine and seek your assistance with this investigation and, if that's not possible, to head off any future violence. The chief is very keen on creating a peaceful community where policing contributes to the maintenance of stability, where people can go about their lawful activities unhampered by villainous behaviour. And to that end, he is encouraging me, as the person implementing his grand plan for the force, to engage with business leaders and support them in whatever way I can so that prosperity returns to our somewhat rundown area.'

Else looked at him and pursed her lips.

'I'll need to speak to my colleagues here to see how we can assist in maintaining the peaceful and stable business environment that you're striving for. I think that we'll probably wish to look at business opportunities in other places, where there is already stability and peacefulness.'

'I can imagine that there are better business opportunities elsewhere in the country,' Iles replied. 'It's been an absolute pleasure to see you again. A real shame you are unable to assist with our investigation, and I suspect we'll have no need to bother you again.'

Harpur and Iles left and drove back to HQ.

Chapter 21

The chief was looking less drawn. He looked out of the window of his office at the frosty grass in the park opposite. He felt jealous of those chiefs who had their HQs in former stately homes, where there was grass, gardens and grand driveways. His office was part of a 1960s office block without aesthetic appeal. But he was happier today.

'It sounds like we've solved a couple of the murders? Looks like Meredith was trying to put some pressure on the dealers and had to deal with a witness. All very tragic for those who died. That leaves us with Meredith's murder.'

'Looked like a professional job,' the head of crime said. 'The Met have spoken to some of his former associates. They have denied knowing anything useful, which is what we expected. However, the feeling at the Met is that things have changed and that they aren't looking to find out who did him in. The Met take is that Meredith was going solo, trying to set up his own dealing network, and that either he was done by someone local here or that they did it themselves. They think that we don't have people capable of doing a job like this around here, so they are looking into their local connections. Of course, it remains our investigation, but they're worried about internal gang violence. They couldn't give a shit about dealers killing each other, but they do have an unfortunate habit of killing the odd, middle-class bystander, and that can get politicians involved.'

'As you say, it's our investigation, so I expect the Met work will be in the line of intelligence gathering. Should anything come to light, I'm sure they'll let us know,' Iles said.

'They really are patronising twats, as if they're the only ones who have professional villains,' the chief said. 'But that does seem to be an end to our investigations, at least for now. I know that we'll keep on investigating to see if anything more can be found out. But I feel comforted that the person who murdered Drummond and Foreshaw poses no future threat and that there is no prospect of further drug-related violence on our streets.'

***

Harpur went to the church where Copsey's life had been commemorated. Copsey's father was there with Pastor Anstruther.

Drummond was looking tired and drawn. He seemed to have shed weight and colour. Profound sadness was etched deeply by the shadows and wrinkles on his face.

'Thank you for coming to see me. Paul's death has left an unfillable hole in my life. I know that nothing you can tell me will fill that void. I blame myself for not trying hard enough to guide him and keep him away from the life that killed him. It's easy to blame others. It's harder to accept blame yourself. I'll have to find a way to live with it.'

Harpur told him about the investigations and how they were resolved.

'Neat solution? Most ends tied up.' Anstruther observed.

'You will have to be able to forgive yourself,' Anstruther said. 'One of my favourite bits of the Bible says "Be kind and compassionate to one another, forgiving each other, just as Christ God forgave you." But we need to add forgiving yourself, too. Paul had wandered away, and you have to allow yourself compassion and understanding.'

After Drummond had gone, Anstruther said to Harpur, 'It was good of you to tell him in person; letters and phones are so impersonal. It does feel a bit too neat, but he's happy that the guy who murdered his son has been dealt with, even if it wasn't by the courts. You've kept the trust, and I thank you for that.'

Harpur shook his hand and left, stepping into the drizzle of early spring.

Chapter 22

Gregory Carmichael sat at the chief's desk. He was wearing a tailored suit of the same quality as those worn by Iles, but grey. He had a white shirt and a mid-blue tie, nothing that might betray any suggestion of personality. He was in his mid-forties. He'd done well to become a permanent secretary at that age.

Swift was sitting in a corner of the office. Harpur, Iles and Davies-Hywel sat in a row in front of the desk.

Carmichael began.

'I think we've reached some conclusions about how the matters involving Inspector Fletcher were dealt with. I thought I could bring you up to date. And here I am sitting in the chief's chair, you'll be thinking, "What's a high-ranking Home Office mandarin doing sitting in the chief's chair?" I don't seek to suggest that I am remotely qualified to be sitting here.'

He threw himself back in the chair and opened his arms wide in acknowledgement of the foolishness of such a suggestion.

'But the chief has been very gracious in allowing me to use his office whilst he is away on holiday. I think I can say, with some confidence, that we have looked into the circumstances in a comprehensive way and can let you know what we have found.'

'Taking everything into account, it seems that the failure to seize, as soon as possible, Mr Fletcher's firearms certificates and, more importantly, as it turned out, his shotguns, was a mistake.'

'Well, that's bleeding obvious with the benefit of hindsight,' Davies-Hywel blurted. 'But all the decisions that were taken were based on the best evidence available at the time they were made. Hindsight makes them look wrong, but at the time they seemed right.'

Carmichael leant forward. The amiability of his expression had vanished, replaced by a narrowing of his eyes and tension in the muscles of his face.

'I note the way you describe the decisions as having been made, without making clear that you were responsible for those decisions. I think we need to be clear that those decisions were your decisions. What was needed here, if I might be quite direct, was foresight, not hindsight.'

Davies-Hywel's face had turned a bright shade of crimson. Spittle sprayed as he spluttered, 'So, so, so you are pinning this all on me? I won't stand for it. Let me tell you, you're in for a fight. The chief was fully informed, and if I'm in the shit, so is he! I made lots of notes. I can show you who knew what and when. No one contradicted my decisions.'

'The notes I've seen make clear that the decisions were delegated to you,' Swift interjected quietly.

'You were there, the pair of you,' Davies-Hywel shouted, turning to Iles and Harpur. 'You know the chief was kept up to date all the way through.'

Harpur decided that this was not the moment to have an opinion, recalling the observation about senior officers knowing when to be absent.

'I remember the chief delegating decisions to command level,' Iles said.

Davies-Hywel abruptly got up and marched out of the office. At the door, he turned and said, 'This is not how this ends. I shall be seeking legal advice. This cannot go unchallenged.'

'That went well,' Carmichael said. 'There's no way to give hard messages other than to be straightforward. The Home Secretary is pleased about the resolution of the other cases and is looking for a similar decisive outcome in this matter. I have, of course, briefed the chief, and he will deal with the situation on his return. It just leaves me to thank you for your support.'

***

Ember, Tacette and Loxton were at the familiar table at The Monty.

'This all looks very rosy, Ralph,' Tacette said.

Loxton nodded vigorously.

'My information is that Meredith is seen as the perpetrator of the Copsey and Foreshaw murders and that they think that Meredith was done by one of his London crew. Brilliant.'

'Professional and experienced,' Ember said, leaning back in a high-backed wooden chair. 'I think the time has come for us to become more, how do I put this, separate. The two jokers from HQ are going to be coming in here, and I don't think it would be too helpful for them to see us cheek by jowl too often. So, much as I love your conversation and general company, I think we need to make this more business-like from here.'

'That's what we loves about you, Ralphy, sorry, Ralph,' Loxton said. 'You foresees all the problems, makes the arrangements and, even though it means sadness in not seeing each other so much, you knows what needs to be done. We'll need to find other ways to have our conversations and conduct our business, but rubbing the cops' noses in it ain't the way to go. Leo and me will have a chat about it and see if we can come up with something better.'

Chapter 23

'So you've got yourself a DCI post then?'

'Yes,' Harpur replied. 'All the pieces fell into place for me. They need someone for the major crimes team after Williams retired. My sergeant at the care team is great, so she can take that on, and I can take up the new job as acting until I can get through a promotion board, assuming I can!'

'Well, yes,' Iles said. 'I hope your interview answers are better than your dress sense.'

The chief walked in, and they both stood.

'Thank you both for the work in the past few days. And thanks in particular to you, Des, for stepping into the acting ACC role. It was not too surprising that Aled felt it was time to retire. I think he had been looking at deputy chief vacancies but concluded that, after such a difficult and demanding year, he needs to spend more time with his family and friends. I would have wished him to stay on to support the implementation of my grand plans for the force, but in many ways, you taking up the ACC role gives more strength to you to lead that work. We'll need a formal promotion board in due course, as we will for new DCIs. Now that all this unpleasantness is behind us, we can look forward to some peace and stability to make the positive changes we need in this force.'